Russia
Arabia
China
Papua New Guinea
Japan
Madagascar
Borneo

Nasty fairy tales from across the globe featuring
real *fairies, horrible trolls, cannibalism,*
bestiality, ghosts, shapeshifters and a changeling child,
amongst other horrors. Adults only.

Viktor Wynd

Stories from Around the World
(That Are Definitely Not Suitable for Children)

illustrated by
Luciana Nedelea

PRESTEL
MUNICH · LONDON · NEW YORK

For the three most beautiful princesses in the world,
Daphne, Phoebe and Leonora, who must not read this book until
they are older. (You will know the stories, for I
have told them to you many times – just not all the details.)

CONTENTS

Viktor Wynd
at his desk –
Suffolk, June 2024

INTRODUCTION

ON FAIRY TALES

Ask me who I am, Ask me who I am
I'm a Tinker, a Deep Tinker

Ask me who I am, Ask me who I am
I'm a Tailor, a Story Tailor

Ask me who I am, Ask me who I am
I'm a Baker, a Master Baker.

I do not know what fairy tales are, where they come from, who wrote them, or who they belong to, but what I *do* know is a lot of stories. I have listened to and learnt stories wherever I have travelled, since I was a child on my grandmother's knee.

People have noses for things that really interest them. Some will always be able to find a good pub, a good restaurant, a football game, a hairdresser, orchids, birds, or even a good TV show. (I rarely watch TV. It's not that I don't like it, it's just that I can't find good things to watch. They do exist, I know – I've seen amazing things on TV – but most of the things I try to watch are boring and bad, and I'd much rather read a book. I can always find a good book.) My nose is for stories. Wherever I go and wherever I look, I seem to find them.

None of the stories in this book are *my* stories; whose they are, I do not know. Sometimes I can tell you when or where I first heard them on my travels, but as I have heard so many of them from different people in different places at different times (and even sometimes read in books), I may not be a reliable witness.

My wife says she doesn't believe a word I say, that I am a congenital liar. *I* say that I am a storyteller; that some people are fraudsters, con men, crooks and bastards, and some people are writers. These stories, I believe, are living things in themselves. They travel from host to host, like a virus. And like a virus, they change and mutate, they re-tell themselves in our heads. Sometimes when I open my mouth to tell a story, I have no idea what will come out or where it came from. The characters seem to be running around inside my head, speaking for themselves, and the story itself takes over. Other times, the story will come out word for word as it was told to me. I don't know how and I don't know why, but that's how it is.

One thing I want you to know is that there is nothing original within these pages. The stories may be horrible, but it is not *my* horror. My editor insists that here I must add an explanation for anything that you may find offensive. I am no Walt Disney and these are no saccharine retellings; they are raw in blood and lust and magic. They may be offensive – indeed they often *are* offensive – but that is the way of the world. What one culture at one time enjoys, another finds repellent.

For example, I will sit on the floor of a Sepik spirit house in New Guinea and eat enormous wriggling sago beetle larvae and I will not judge (even if it is not my favourite dish in the world – there's always a taste there that somehow reminds me of poo, and I'm not so keen on things wriggling in my mouth… well, not so keen on my *food* wriggling in my mouth, at any rate). So I will listen to stories, and I will not judge.

Please, gentle reader, remember that these stories were around before we were born and will be around long after we are dead. If you are of a timid disposition, do not read. If you *enjoy* being offended, read on. But please, I pray of you, do not be offended with *me* – accept my apologies. These are not my stories, not my sins; they've all happened, all will happen again.

In these stories, there may be monsters, and they may or may not be of the Other World. Those from the Other World might be easier to understand, but as we all know well, within churches and schools, strange country houses and behind firmly-locked doors lurk all manner of evils. So if we venture back to the time of these stories, a time without the modern state and concept of law universally applied, these evils must be magnified.

There ought to be fairies in a fairy tale, I think. They don't always have them, but as long as they have an ogre, a shapeshifter, or a magical being, I will be content. Most societies across the world have these creatures, and in many places I travel, they are as real to the locals as double-decker buses or post boxes are to us Brits. I think, indeed I *know*, that they are all real. For the purpose of this book I will merely say that a fairy tale is one in which people interact with the Other World in some shape or form, though there may be a story or two that takes place wholly there. We will see. Fairy tales flow with the logic of dreams. People, things, places, all come and go for no apparent reason – but in their own world, they make perfect sense.

Wherever I have been in the world I have heard stories, and I have always been a traveller (or a tourist; I am quite happy with either designation). When I was a child, there was a vast map of the world on the kitchen wall of my parents' North London flat – though we only ventured as far as the continent a handful of times. I, meanwhile, looked at the map and dreamt. I read every book that Gerald Durrell and David Attenborough had written. I read travellers' tales, from Ibn Battuta to John Mandeville. There was a huge world out there that I wanted to see when I was older (before becoming Robert Musil, Salvador Dalí and world king, rolled into one).

The first choice I was given as an almost-adult was what to study at university. I chose Islamic history at London's School of Oriental and African Studies. True, it was not travelling, but it was all about the far away world. I lived frugally in a tiny room in a council flat and saved up so I could visit the places I'd only read about. I've been travelling ever since, and learning stories. My feet are itchy; I cannot sit still.

In 2018 I started my travel agency, Gone with the Wynd, because I needed to travel, and the places I wanted to go to and the things I wanted to do were too expensive to go to alone. You need guides, porters, cooks, boats and cars, and the cost for one person is not much different as for six. I cannot afford to go alone, so I take people, and I try to go to places where few, if any, other agencies go, specialising in New Guinea and West Africa. I have spent my whole life dreaming of these places, but why do so few people want to come with me? (Conversely, those that do come say it's because they don't have any friends that like to travel.) The truth is that people who *need* to travel, travel. They will always find a way.

For people like me, travelling and collecting interesting things are linked psychological conditions. My home has long since filled up, so I have a museum in east London called the Viktor Wynd Museum of Curiosities, Fine Art & UnNatural History, now equally overflowing with wonders. When I have to be in England, I can look (you can come and look with me) at my treasures and travel in my mind. But I digress: I don't want to lose you, dear gentle reader. Come with me to fairy land – turn the page and start my book.

(If there are any children reading this, they need to stop now. This is not a Ladybird book; these are not tales for young and tender ears.)

HOW TO USE THIS BOOK

In olden days, the storyteller took the place of yesterday's books and today's television; everyone listened to us and we were everywhere. In the sad, gloomy and lifeless modern world, we have been displaced. But we are still there if you go looking for us, surviving on the edges.

Some say that to write a story down kills it. I don't agree, as long as no one thinks that there is a correct version of a tale, and there are no qualifications. Anyone can, and indeed *should*, tell stories, no audience needed (though it can be rather nice).

I would like this book to be used in a certain way, my dear gentle reader. I would be delighted if you lay in bed and read it to yourself at night. But really, you should first read it aloud to the person next to you, on the phone to a friend, or to your cat. (Do not worry if the person looks bored, or even falls asleep. I tell my children stories until they fall asleep. I tell my wife stories, though perhaps she only pretends to be asleep in the hope that I will shut up. I tell strangers stories, though of course it is the stories that are using me as a vessel to tell themselves.)

Next, you should tell the story to someone without the book being there. Let it live in your mind, let it tell itself, and let it come out as a whole new story – or perhaps it is the same story.

At the end of the book are some instructions for telling stories. You shouldn't need them; it should be innate. But sometimes, a nudge is as good as a wink.

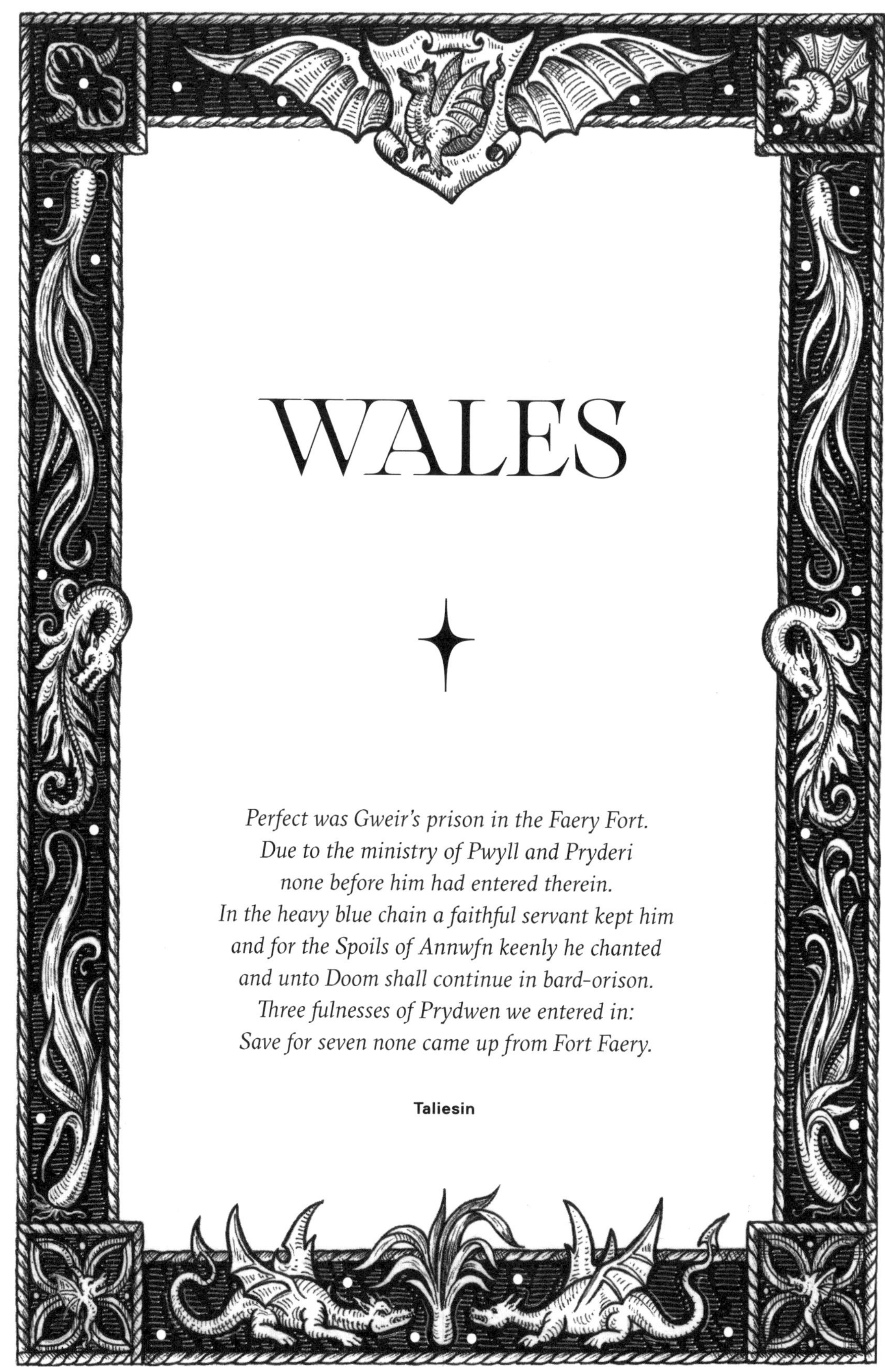

WALES

Perfect was Gweir's prison in the Faery Fort.
Due to the ministry of Pwyll and Pryderi
none before him had entered therein.
In the heavy blue chain a faithful servant kept him
and for the Spoils of Annwfn keenly he chanted
and unto Doom shall continue in bard-orison.
Three fulnesses of Prydwen we entered in:
Save for seven none came up from Fort Faery.

Taliesin

Memories from when I am very small are vague. Some are as clear as yesterday. Others have been told and retold among my family so many times that it's not always clear if I am remembering the actual event or just its discussion; if the vision in my mind comes from memory or just from photographs.

I do remember that I only visited my great-grandmother Topsy in Wales once. She lived in a tiny cottage high in the hills above Harlech in Snowdonia. I can see it now. Even though it was summer, it was raining. It might only have been five miles from the caravan park by the dunes where we stayed, but it took over an hour of twisting, turning lanes, of opening gates and driving through fields of sheep, to get there.

The cottage was nestled in the mountains, and smoke came out of the chimney. We parked and crossed the ancient stone hearth. It was made up of two rooms, with a fireplace in the centre that heated them both. One room held a bed, a great sofa, some faded black-and-white family photos of grim-looking people in black suits, a rocking chair and a great wardrobe. We went into the other room – the kitchen – to sit around the table. (Or rather, first to the loo – it was a long drive and I was a small boy. I remember the loo because, even in those days, it was unusual for it to be outside. I also remember the cottage as being without electricity or running water, but my older brother says this is nonsense, it couldn't have had a loo and not had running water. Besides, there was a sink in the kitchen. Where I remember a cauldron over a fire, he remembers a coal-fired kitchen stove with an oven and a hot top where the kettle boiled.) The rest I have heard so many times at family gatherings, to much laughter, that either it must be true or it must be a good story – but I'm not sure that I remember it.

My father had to remind his grandmother who he was. She grunted, then he said he'd brought her newest great-grandson – me – to visit. She grunted again and said, 'Let's have a look at him.' Then she said something to me in Welsh. I didn't reply, so she turned to my father and, in English, asked if I spoke Welsh. 'Of course not, Granny,' he replied. She turned her back on me and supposed that my parents would like a cup of tea. She'd never been interested in my father, because, he said, he did not speak Welsh and she hated the English. (Which is odd because it is not a common Welsh sentiment. However, once upon a time she had had an English husband and he, family memory says, was not very nice.) My brother and I played in the stream and then we drove back to the caravan. My father said we'd spent more time driving there and back than with her, and we didn't need to see her again. She'd never liked him and wasn't interested in us anyway.

We didn't go to Harlech again. Instead we went to the Brecon Beacons. We'd camp in Farmer Davies's field, the same field my father had camped in with his friends when he was at the university. When it rained, which it seemed to do more often than not, Mrs Davies would invite us into the fine old farmhouse with slate floor to sit by the fire in the kitchen and eat toasted teacakes or buttered toast. Sometimes, the farmer's mother, old Mrs Davies, would be there, and she used to tell us stories: stories of dragons, Pwyl, Pryderi, Manawydan and Merlin. One particularly wet summer, when it rained like it had never rained before, I spent a lot of time with old Mrs Davies and filled an exercise book with her stories – but then my tent flooded, and the book was ruined. Some of these stories I remember her first telling me when I was a little boy. Others I have picked up along the way.

Two last memories I have of Wales as a child: my first sight of a yellow wagtail, bobbing and waving on the rocks in the stream, and high tea at the farm. Young Mrs Davies brought a great dish of roast potatoes to the table and, looking at me, said, 'You don't like these, do you?' But oh how I *loved*, and still love, roast potatoes. Sarcasm is wasted on children.

Viktor Wynd's
great-grandmother's cottage
Cwm Croesor,
1980.

Our little girl does not want to go down the mine.
The Christian does not want the little people – the pooka – to be fed.
But who will have the power? Who will have the glory?

The Pooka and the Old Ways Triumph Over the Christian

ong, long ago – perhaps as long ago as the time the blessed saints Julian and Aaron were martyred – the people of Great Orme, next to what is now Llandudno, were copper miners. Life was hard on the grim north coast of Wales. It was not possible to scratch a good living from farming, but scratching down beneath the rocks, they'd found copper. Everyone worked down the mines and everyone lived well, but they did not work alone, for the pooka lived in the mines and helped them. I can't describe a pooka because I have never seen one, but they are still about, I'm told. Every description I have ever heard is different. Some say they are very small; others say they are very big. They are like us, but they are not us. They change their shapes and become animals, but when they look like us, there's often something slightly wrong – they're mischievous, they think in the moment, act quickly – so perhaps they'll still be all covered with fur, have a tail, a hare's ears, a dog's nose, or some other thing about them that makes you realise they are of the otherworld.

Since time immemorial, the pooka had guided the miners by tapping the ground where rich seams of copper could be found. If someone got lost in the labyrinthine maze or their lamp went out, the pooka would tap them up to the surface. It was a mutually beneficial relationship. Long ago a deal had been done via elaborate and secret rituals wherein, every week, a different family of initiated miners prepared a feast. The offerings varied with the seasons: a lamb or deer might be roasted, special cakes made, jams delivered, loaves baked.

On that fateful day, a man dressed in rags came to the village. They treated him as they treated all strangers, with courtesy and respect. They even let him build a hut in the woods and gave him food. He would talk to them about a new god – a god that was not just one god, but was three gods, but was also one god. A god that demanded that they drink its blood and eat its flesh. A god who would grant them many things. A god that had hardly been seen since the beginning of time, but who had a son who had been seen, and been killed by some people far away, yet had not *really* been killed. On top of this nonsense (for *their* gods died all the time and didn't make much fuss about it, just simply reappeared), he said that they were all sinners, and guilty of the murder of this man/god who hadn't really died? They took him for another travelling fool and hoped he'd go away soon, not that there was any harm in him. And as for all his words against the pooka, well, he was a madman, was he not?

Unfortunately, there was one girl in the village, Winnifred, who listened to him. She was terrified of the mine. She hated it, and knew that in a couple of years, she would have to join everyone else underground with the dreadful pooka. She liked the sound of this new god, and she asked him to get rid of the copper and the pooka, so she wouldn't have to go underground. Her brother Owen had recently been initiated, and when it was his turn to help prepare and take the family feast down the mines, Winnifred said that she would take it for him. He laughed at this; he loved his sister dearly and knew how she hated the mines – but she pointed out how tired and exhausted he was. Truth to tell, he *was* tired and exhausted, and had been down the mines already once that day. The time would come soon enough when she would have to join him, so she might as well get used to it.

Winnifred took the offerings straight to the man in rags, and they both laughed and feasted on it themselves (they couldn't eat it all, but he said he'd eat the rest another time). Tomorrow, he said, there would still be plenty of copper, and then he would preach again, such a sermon on the wickedness of giving food to non-existent magical troglodytes that he would convert them all. But, alas, there was no copper the next day, nothing but long, worried faces. Owen asked Winnifred if she'd left the offerings, and she said of course she had. However, all week there was no copper. Everyone looked grimmer and grimmer, and her brother started to worry that there had been something wrong with the ritual since it was his first time, and he had been tired and exhausted. As time went on and no copper was found, people began to talk of the days before the accommodation had been reached with the pooka, when they'd sacrificed young men to them. People in the village began to talk of Owen. It must have been something he'd done, they said.

On the night of the full bilberry moon, Winnifred woke up with the feeling something was wrong. She leant over to nudge her brother, but he wasn't there. She knew in an instant that he had gone to offer himself as a sacrifice in the mine, and she knew that that was wrong. If anyone had to be sacrificed, it would be her. Taking a lamp, she ran to the mine, her heart filled with horror and fear. She went in and she went down, down, down until, deep in the mine, she turned a corner and her lamp went out. She threw herself on the floor and began to cry. She felt she was not alone; she knew something – or someone – was with her, and it filled her with horror. She could barely breathe. It was a not a friendly something, but it was definitely a *something*, and not a *someone*, and it was coming for her.

She screamed out and begged that they take her and let her brother live. It was her fault, she said, she'd been led astray, but it wasn't her brother's fault. She cried, 'Take me, take me, not him. It was my doing.' She said the offerings would continue just as before, 'But don't kill Owen, kill me.' And then, just like that, she felt she was alone. She didn't know what to do. She tried to walk but didn't know where, so she stopped. After what seemed an age, but might have been a minute (well, probably not a minute, but not an hour either), she heard a tapping, a friendly tapping, and she went to it.

The tapping led on down shaft after shaft, deep, deep into the earth, until in the far distance she saw a faint glow and found Owen with a broken leg. Then the tapping started again, and putting her brother's arm around her shoulders, she supported Owen all the way out of the mine.

The next day, the tapping started again. Copper was found, and a huge feast was prepared and taken to the pooka. People were not cross with Winnifred – it was not her fault, she had been led astray – but they *were* cross with the man in rags. And I won't tell what they did to him, but I know it was not a nice thing, or things. For his sake, let us hope he joined saints Julian and Aaron in another world and lived happily ever after. The pooka were very pleased and got a special treat they had not had for many centuries.

In which a little boy with no parents and no friends starts working for a witch (which is not always a good idea). Will the boy escape, even if he becomes a hare? Or will the witch eat the boy (which may not always be a bad thing)?

Gwion Bach

nce upon a time, in a small town in a small valley, a boy named Gwion Bach appeared. None knew his father and none knew his mother. Perhaps they were dead. Perhaps he was someone's bastard son. Perhaps he'd been abandoned. None knew, and to be perfectly honest, none cared. An urchin boy was an urchin boy. He could sleep where he liked...well, not in *their* shed, or they'd beat him. He could eat what he wanted...but not from *their* apple tree, or they'd beat him. Unless, that is, they needed help with the picking, when they'd send him up the tallest ladder and then let him take some apples as payment. He had no home, so he slept where he could. He had no one to feed him, so he ate where he could. But he was a nice boy, and helpful, so he wasn't chased out of town. Indeed, if he hadn't kept asking questions all the time, he would have been a useful nuisance whenever errands were needed. But he *would* ask questions, all the time: why is fire hot? Why does the sun come out every day and the moon but once a month? Why is it always raining? Why is the grass green? How do the daffodils know when to grow? Why are sheep round and fluffy? Why are leeks so tasty? Why are the English always so ugly, and why does no one go near the cave by the lake? 'Because that's where the evil witch lives, who eats boys like you for breakfast – now shut up and fuck off!'

The problem was that, wherever he went, if people didn't want him for something, they'd tell him to go away and throw stones at him, so there weren't so many places that he could go. One spring, as the Lent lilies were coming up, he found himself by the lake. It was a big lake, and the cave was by the far side. If he hadn't been so busy with his thoughts and trying to work out why water was wet, he would never have got so close. It was then that he saw the woman walking by the lake. He would never have guessed that she was a witch if she hadn't been wearing a tall, peaked hat. Every now and again she stooped down to gather things or reached up to take a feather from a bird's nest. She caught a newt, gently took out one of its eyes and put it back, chopped a toe off a frog, plucked a bat from the air and cut off its wool, grabbed an adder and took its tongue. Gulping, he looked left and right but there was nowhere to hide, so he dashed into the woods going up the mountain behind him and hid inside the hollow trunk of an enormous oak.

Gwion Bach felt something cold and clammy running over him, and he knew she was looking at the wood. The feeling passed, and he hoped she was looking at something else...but then it came back, it came back tenfold. He was covered in goose bumps. There was no *way* she could see him there, but the feeling wasn't going away.

'Boy, reach into the hole in the tree beside you and bring me a baby owl,' she suddenly commanded. Without knowing how, or even needing to tell his body what to do, he reached into the hole and took an owlet. Then he found himself in front of her and she took the bird, ripped off a wing and put in in her bag.

'Who are you?' she demanded in a fury.

'Gwion Bach.'

'What are you doing in my wood? How dare you come here?' If her eyes could kill – which they couldn't – he'd have been dead by now. He felt very small and very, very afraid.

'Who is your father?'

'I haven't got a father.'

'Who is your mother?'

'I don't have a mother.'

'Well, who looks after you?'

'Nobody looks after me.'

The witch suddenly changed. She went from being a furious figure who looked as though she was going to chop him up and put him in the pot for dinner to a kindly old lady, greeting her long-lost and favourite grandchild. Gwion was suspicious. Only the other day, the butcher had seen him taking a pie, smiled and said, 'You poor thing, you must be really hungry, come and have another,' and then, when he'd trotted happily back to take it, whacked him hard across the face and told him that he ever caught him stealing pies again, he would end up in a pie himself. And the butcher meant it.

Still, Gwion felt he couldn't run away. Even if he'd wanted to, his legs would not obey. The witch explained that she wasn't an evil witch, she just liked to be left alone (and to do her, and indeed most witches, justice, there was nothing evil about her, but people – by which I mean men – won't leave single women alone). She grabbed a lizard, snipped its leg off with a pair of scissors, popped it in her bag and said, 'Never mind dear, it will soon grow back.' (Although this isn't really true. Some amphibians – notably the axolotl – can regrow limbs, but not lizards. They can only regrow their tails. Though I suppose she was a witch, so either she didn't know, or she was comforting the lizard, or using her magic so that it could regrow.)

No, she *was not* and *did not want to be* a wise woman. But she *could* be. She could've been the best, but she had her mind on other things. And the only way she could get people to leave her alone was by pretending to be a bad witch, or so she explained, as she talked kindly to Gwion Bach whilst feeding him a delicious apple pie that she just so happened to have in her pocket. Gwion had no love or respect for society and felt he understood. So when she asked him if he'd like to come and work for her – she'd pay him a penny a day and feed him all he could eat, if he would but stir a cauldron for a year and a day – he was not terrified, but asked how he could stir without stopping for so long? 'Not to worry,' the witch replied; she herself could stir at night when he was asleep. In the day she needed to gather offerings for the cauldron, which was not, she assured him, evil. Then there was Mrs Morgan, the housekeeper, who could cover now and again during the day when he needed a little break, to eat perhaps.

It was an offer no hungry, homeless, friendless orphan could refuse. He wasn't sure exactly how much a penny was, or how many days there were in a year, but in his short life he'd never had all the food he could eat. He trotted happily back to the cave and set to stirring the cauldron. Then, for a moment, the witch looked like an evil witch again. She told him that if he so much as tasted the potion, he'd be put in the pot and she would eat him – and he knew that she would, even if she didn't want to. Even if, as she said, she'd never eaten a boy before, never even *thought* of eating a boy. And if she was going to start eating boys, she wouldn't start with a skinny wretch like him, oh no, she'd start with Bill the butcher's boy, who was famously rotund. Gwion suspected then that perhaps she had thought of eating boys before, because even he had thought about eating Bill.

Gwion loved his new life. Mrs Morgan was wonderful. She would come and chat for hours and was always feeding him. The witch herself was rather a sweetheart, telling him long stories about her childhood, and every now and then making him a particularly delicious cake. He had never had enough to eat, never slept in the same place twice, never been with people who liked him, never felt himself useful before – and every day, the pile of pennies grew. He went from being a skinny boy to being rather a fat boy, but it didn't worry him. He felt like one of the family.

One day, he looked out of the cave and saw the Lent lilies were about to bloom. When he'd started stirring they'd been blooming, so it must be coming up to a year and a day. He looked at his great pile of pennies. He had no idea how many there were, but it was an awful lot. He'd be able to buy all the butcher's pies (not that they were as nice as the witch's pies). No, he'd go to the baker and buy all the baker's cakes...no, they wouldn't be as good as the witch's. No, what he *really* needed was a house. He'd buy himself a house, and clothes. He had no idea how much that would cost but he had an awful lot of pennies. As the delicious thoughts tumbled through his mind his attention slipped, and he splashed some of the cauldron's broth onto his hand. It was hot, *so* hot. He screamed, wiped it on his trousers and tried to lick it better, but in licking it he tasted the forbidden fruit.

And all of a sudden, he knew why the potion was hot: it had been heated by fire that had come from the mouth of the very first

dragon and been passed around mankind ever since. He knew that the moon was pulling the daffodils out of the land. And he knew that the witch was coming and that the witch would chop him up and put him in the cauldron and eat him, and he knew that if he ran to the back of the cave and pushed the big stone, there was a passage only he could fit down and escape, and he knew the witch had shrunk and come up after him, and he knew he was a fat round boy and couldn't run very fast and the witch was going to catch him, and he knew that if he was a hare he could run faster than her, and he *was* a hare, and he was getting away, but the witch was now a greyhound and he knew she could run faster than him, but he knew that a greyhound could not swim and if he leapt into the lake and was a fish he could escape, and he was a fish. And the witch was an otter, and he knew there was nowhere he could swim that the otter couldn't catch him. And he knew if he was a pigeon, he could fly away and the otter couldn't follow, and he was a pigeon, and he knew the witch was a gyrfalcon soaring high above and that she was coming for him, and he could not escape unless he was a worm and could crawl underground and then he'd be safe. At least, he *would* be safe, if the witch were not a mole waiting underground to gobble him up.

Nine months later, the witch gave birth to a boy. Much as she loved him, she knew someone else would love him more. She wrapped him warmly and put him in a coracle that floated down the river, where he was found by a prince who named him Taliesin, and he grew to be the greatest poet the world has ever known.

The complicated adventures of an unloved girl called Gwen, her horrible childhood, an enchanted valley, the witch that wants to eat her, the farmer that wants to kill her and the boy who wants to marry her.

Gwen, the Pig and the Witch

In Powys long, long ago, so long ago that no one's quite sure when it was, but everyone agrees that it did happen, indeed there is no *question* about whether it happened or not – for it is a story and all stories are true, and all stories have happened (now, whether they happened to the actual people in them at the time the story says they did is another matter)...but anyhow. At the time this tale begins, there was a servant wench, Branwen, at the great Cold Comfort Farm, who gave birth to a girl she called Gwendolyn. It could have been a miracle, for she was unmarried and 'no one knew' who the father was. Which is to say that *everyone* knew who the father was. It was her master, Farmer Evens, who'd done something nasty to her in the woodshed. But everyone was afraid of him, and no one dared face up to him, for he was friends with that evil English Magistrate Smith and could have anyone locked up. Not that he'd need to when he could take his whip to you, *did* take his whip to you – and especially to his wife, Rhiannon, who might or might not have said something about this new baby, but was so roundly whipped that Farmer Evens then had to do his own milking for at least a week.

As he was milking, he looked long and hard at the cow's bottom in front of his face and came to the conclusion that a cow's bottom was a much more trouble-free area of pleasure than serving wenches.

Oh, he knew all about sheep, don't worry about that. But he had sworn an oath that he would only go down on his knees twice in his life – once before God and once before entering a woman – and he was not going to go down on his knees before, or rather behind, a sheep. Oh no, he'd much rather stand on a stool behind a cow. Besides, there was always a cow in the barn, whereas sheep had to be caught. True, the cow boy Billy had asked him if he preferred Esmerelda or Maude, but he'd whipped Billy and made him have a go, only to discover that Billy was actually rather partial to Maude. So he'd whipped Billy again for good measure and they hadn't talked about it any further, though Farmer Evens stuck to Esmerelda from there on.

As you have probably guessed by now, Farmer Evens was not a nice man, and his farm was not a nice place to be. Branwen's life was not a good life, not a happy life. Her daughter, Gwen, was not welcome at the farm, but as she was born there, they'd feed her and make her useful. Branwen's life was already miserable, but Gwen only made it worse. There was some motherly instinct that meant that, while Branwen did look after her daughter, she was never nice to her.

When Gwen was twelve, she came running to her mother to say that the master's son, George Evens (and no good could be expected of anyone with an English name like George, could it?), was threatening to be nice to her. Branwen shrugged and explained that they were poor people. It always had been the lot of the poor to service the rich and it always would be. They were just cattle after all, and everyone knew that what the Evenses did with their cattle, they'd do with their servants. Gwen would just have to get used to it.

'Don't try and enjoy it,' her mother said. 'There's no fun to be had from that sort of thing for a girl. Just do your best to keep his purple-headed womb ferret in your back hole, then you won't have a baby. He's a nasty boy, that George, I'll give you that. Why can't he just stick to the sheep? The rich are all the same! Let them burn in hell – but I'll bet they'll find a way of taking their gold with them down there and making us carry on looking after them. Preacher Jones may well say there's a special place in hell for the rich and the English, that there'll be red-hot pokers going up their arses all day long. I don't believe it. I think *they'll* be the ones with the pokers and *we'll* still be the ones with the arses. Either that or they'll enjoy it.

They'll probably enjoy it! I once saw Magistrate Smith and Farmer Jones taking it in turns to put their nightsticks up each other's bottoms and they looked like they were enjoying it, alright. But then they saw me watching them, grabbed me, and that's when one of them – or both of them, I don't remember which – ended up in my front bottom, and I don't know which one of them is your father.'

Gwen did not want George Evens to put his disgusting thing in any of her holes, and the only way she could see of avoiding it was to run away. Young George was the only person who would miss her, and he wouldn't *really* miss her – he had his sheep, after all. To be honest, he really loved his sheep.* He'd just thought Gwen would make a change once in a while, that's all. Well, Branwen would have to do, she'd make a change. He couldn't try a cow; his father had smacked him 'round the face when he'd caught him looking at Esmerelda. (...I am writing this story but it's not *my* story, so there isn't much I can do to change things. However, as Gwen has walked out of the farm and the valley forever, I can set fire to that farmhouse and we can watch them all being burnt to death, good riddance to bad rubbish. I can't control what will happen to them in hell, but I *can* confirm it involves red-hot pokers. I very much hope they don't enjoy it, though the rich are so strange I really wouldn't put anything past them.)

That summer's day, Gwen set out and walked across the horizon. Somehow, growing up surrounded by sadists who hated her had not spoilt her character. She was a good girl, but she had learnt how to survive and had developed a very powerful sense of danger. She knew who to beg from and who not, who might help her and

* When I have told this story to urban audiences, they have sometimes been shocked, or even disgusted, by certain details. Rural audiences, however, tend to find it more amusing, with various nudges and winks rippling through them. Indeed, at one agricultural show where I was telling tales (I won't say which, otherwise I won't be booked again), the audience was particularly raucous – it was next to the cider tent. I well remember a stout, forbidding lady leaning over to her teenage son and whispering in his ear, 'See what I told you! You leave them girls alone. There ain't nothing you can do with them you can't do with one of 'em sheep!' She was whispering too loudly, for the whole tent heard and roared with laughter – apart from the boy, who turned bright red, whereupon a red-faced farmer turned to his wife and said, 'Why there you go, Beryl, I always told you what that Tom does with the cows in the milking shed ain't nothing to be ashamed of, and saves us having to go in there at three in the morning!'

who would not. She knew only too well that the prosperous, round-faced, smiling people were best avoided. And whilst there was good reason for society to shun some people (had not Farmer Evens been shunned by everyone but the magistrate in his valley?), those they looked askance at – the ugly ones, the deformed ones or, more simply, those without social graces – were often, but not always, the kindest ones. She'd never had a day off in her life, never had a day when she hadn't been shouted at or slapped and made to scrub the floor, to clean out the pigs, or been shut in the pigsty overnight as a punishment for not scrubbing hard enough. She loved her freedom, and she loved her world. Wales was, and always would be, the most beautiful place on earth. Just to be there, to hear the birds sing and the brooks bubble, to see the mountains clothed in oak and hazel rearing up all around filled her with joy.

That was the best summer of her life. She slept in hedges, made friends with nice people who fed her, avoided nasty people who might have done her harm, skipped and ran, turned cartwheels, sang, climbed trees, threw stones and made fires. But she knew it couldn't last, that autumn and winter would come, that it would rain almost every day (or rather, that it would *continue* to rain and get very cold). She'd need to find somewhere where they would be kind to a poor orphan bastard girl, and that was not easy to come by. Her powerful sense for danger kept alerting her wherever she went.

Finally she saw a valley in the distance and it called to her. She did not know why, but she was drawn to it. The very grass seemed greener, the trees taller, the brook bubblier, the cows and the sheep fatter. She was filled with a sense of goodness and safety as she walked up. She made her way towards a great farm surrounded by orchards laden with fruit and asked a passing labourer about the farmer, and whether he thought she'd be able to get any sort of place there.

'Oh no, don't go there, not on your nelly,' she was told. The farm belonged to a horrible rich Englishman, Richard Peak ('Well not by rights it didn't!'). His sister had married Farmer Pwyl and had a boy, the young master Llewelyn, and all had been wonderful, but then Richard Peak had come to visit and first the parents had disappeared and then the boy, and there was nothing they could do, the labourer explained. The local magistrate was English as well, and friends with the new master. They would all have left, but it was their home, and where would they go? And then the master might come back and all would be right again, wouldn't it?

Gwen realised that if she didn't go now, he'd never stop talking. Besides, she liked the valley, she felt it in her bones, and just because the master was English it didn't automatically mean he was bad. It could just be another one of those silly prejudices. She knocked at the great door. The farmer came out, looked her up and down and sneered. She could feel he was a bad man, but at least he wasn't looking at her the way George Evens had. He had no job for her; no she couldn't have an apple – that would be stealing, and the magistrate would hang her for it. One thing she could do was 'BUGGER OFF.' But she wanted to stay. She'd had a bad master before. She could live with it, it was so beautiful. She wouldn't need paying, she said.

'I should think not, a little girl like you.'

'There must be something I can do,' she pleaded.

'Well if you can find me the seven golden leaves, then you can stay. Now get off my land, bugger off.'

Well she'd tried, tried her hardest. There was bound to be another farm. She followed the river up the valley and sat down for a rest under a great oak tree with enormous curling roots. She looked at the roots and saw something that only a child could see: the roots seemed to form a face. Then she did something that only a child would do: she said hello, and the roots said hello back. They got into a conversation, and as she talked, the roots slowly moved around and formed themselves into a little man who hopped up and sat beside her, one of the Fair Folk. (Now, it is said that only children can speak with the Fair, for they are closer to their size. But this is nonsense because the Fair have no natural size. Sometimes they are big, sometimes they are small. We rarely notice them when they're big, for they walk with us. Perhaps we notice the ears, or the setting of the face, but that too can change. It is said that they aren't as common as they used to be, but that's not true; it's just that they are very good at hiding and we are very bad at looking. Children may see them more often, but children are using their eyes to look and see what their eyes see, not what society trains their brains to expect their eyes to see. But I digress, and it is only thanks to my beautiful editor that there is any story here at all.

She has already removed over 80 per cent of my peregrinations. Even now, her red pen hovers over this paragraph: gentle reader, if I don't get back to the story right away, we will run out of pages and you will never find out what happens to our dear Gwen.)

As was her way, Gwen made firm friends with the little fellow. All went well until, in jest, she asked him if he knew where the seven golden leaves were? He fell off his root onto the ground, became deadly pale and immediately started talking noisily about the weather, so she asked again. He thought it looked like rain. She asked again, and he wasn't so sure if it was going to rain today but thought if it didn't it would most definitely rain tomorrow. She asked again, and he said that it was lovely to meet her, but he really must be going. So she asked *again*. Reluctantly, he looked from left to right and said that he would whisper the story to her. He turned into a rat and climbed onto her shoulder. Then he turned into a cricket and jumped up inside her ear. Then he became an earwig, sat down and whispered the story of the Seven Golden Leaves.

At the beginning of time, the world had been one large black rock. Then lightning had struck here in the valley and a silver birch grew. Lightning struck the birch and seven golden leaves grew. Then lightning struck the ground and the first of the Fair Folk appeared. He'd climbed the trees, picked the seven golden leaves and wished for a wife and for plants to eat. Then, when they were bored of plants, they'd wished for animals. When they were bored of each other, they'd wished for children. When the children grew up, they'd wished for grandchildren. And so it was that the whole world was wished into existence in that very valley, which was why it was the richest, most beautiful valley in the whole world. Unfortunately there were just seven leaves, and unfortunately not all the Fair Folk were that good at wishing, because they had also wished people into existence. Then someone, perhaps a child, had thought it was a good idea to wish for a witch to add some spice to their life. This witch had got hold of the leaves and had gone on to wish for all sorts of wicked things, like money and hunger and cold and the English. (Though her Fair little friend wasn't sure if the witch really knew how to wish new things into being, for if the Fair Folk had wished for a witch, they could surely have wished for the other bad things too – but not the English; only a really wicked witch could have wished for them.)

The wicked witch lived high up in the valley and ate children. Like a spider, she didn't need to eat all the time, maybe only once a decade. But when she did, the valley always gave her one. It was the price they had to pay for being there, for all the bounties the valley gave them. No, he said, Gwen was *not* to go up the valley, she should go back the way she came and leave for good. 'Well it's been very nice chatting, but I really do have to go now, bye bye.' He leapt out of her ear, turned back into a rat, climbed down, turned back into a little man, bowed and disappeared back into the tree roots. Gwen got up and set off down the valley. Then she stopped, sat down and started to think. She had never, ever, in all her life done anything useful, never had a purpose, never been able to help others. This was her chance. She turned around and marched up the valley.

She hadn't gone far when she came to a little cottage. It was the prettiest cottage she had ever seen. The garden was full of flowers, roses, hollyhocks, snowdrops, daffodils, dahlias, daisies and lilies (I know they shouldn't have been all flowering at once, but they were). It was so pretty, so very pretty, that Gwen knew it must be a good place, a happy place. And so it was. She went up the path, knocked on the door and the kindest, most loving old lady was there. She was everyone's dream of the perfect grandmother. She smiled kindly on our Gwen and was very sorry, no, she didn't have any work – but would she like a piece of apple pie? It was the most delicious thing Gwen had ever eaten. No, there was nothing further up the valley except for a horrible witch in a peaked hat, with a nose that met her chin, who lived there and ate children. What Gwen should do was leave the valley and find a place elsewhere.

Yet they carried on chatting. Gwen finished the apple pie. The kind old lady wondered if she'd like to have some sausages and told her to call her Mother Nancy. And then, as it was getting dark, she supposed it would be alright if Gwen slept by the hearth, as long as she didn't mind sleeping next to a pig? Now as it happened, if there was one thing Gwen hated it was pigs. She'd been made to clean the pigsties since she had been able to walk, made to sleep with them often enough as a punishment. She hated them: hated their smell, hated their turned-up, arrogant noses. She had sworn that she would never, *ever* again have anything to do with pigs. But the old lady was kind, and it wasn't her fault, and it was getting dark, and she didn't want to go out at night with that wicked witch about, so holding her nose, she slept with the pig.

The next morning she was given an enormous breakfast of fried eggs, bacon, sausages, black pudding, beans and toast. They set to talking, and it was as if the old lady really was her grandmother and she the favourite long-lost granddaughter. The old lady got some bread rolls and filled them with ham and cheese for Gwen's journey, gave her a warm scarf and a handful of small coins, went with her to the front gate to say goodbye and make sure that she walked off down the valley, not up to the witch. But, what with one thing or another, they never actually said goodbye.

Old Mother Nancy explained that she liked living alone, had always wanted to live alone. Ever since, as a child, she'd seen the bull with the cow at her parents' farm, she'd sworn no man was *ever* getting near her and that was why she'd lived here. But now that she was old, she wished she'd had a child – if only there'd been a way of having a child that didn't involve a man, she said. They both shuddered at the thought. She didn't have any work for Gwen, but winter was coming, she felt the cold in her bones. Someone had to take the pig out into the woods every day, and if Gwen didn't mind, she could stay till spring. But she was only to walk the pig in the woods below the cottage, mind, and never to go up the valley, for that was where the witch lived (not that the witch would be that interested in Gwen. She preferred children, and Gwen was probably too old for her). She couldn't pay anything but could feed her and keep her warm. Gwen was happy, perhaps the happiest she'd ever been. She hugged the old lady and was hugged back. It was the first hug she'd ever had in her life, and she liked it. There was only one fly in the ointment, and that fly was a rather large porcine creature called Piggy. But overall, she was extremely happy.

She took Piggy for his walks every day, keeping her distance. She was much happier back at the cottage chattering away with Mother Nancy, eating her endless supplies of cakes, bread, cheese, sausages and pies. The pig, however, kept coming up to her and nuzzling her.

He was one of those pigs with a stripe down its back, and eventually, even Gwen had to admit he was quite a handsome pig, condescending to scratch him once in a while, which seemed to give him so much pleasure. One night after Mother Nancy had gone upstairs to bed, Gwen stayed awake by the fire thinking about how lucky she was, how happy she was. Then she looked at the pig and her heart was filled with pity; it was such a stupid creature. So stupid it probably didn't even know it *was* stupid (not that stupid people do know they're stupid either). She scratched the pig and looked into his eyes, saying, 'Poor pig, you are so stupid, so very stupid, and ugly and you smell.'

'Oy! Who are you calling stupid?' snapped the pig. 'And whilst we are on the subject, I don't suppose anyone has ever called you pretty' (which of course they hadn't. Not that she wasn't pretty – as it happens, she wasn't – but even if she had been, no one would have noticed). 'And when did *you* last have a bath?'

Gwen sat up amazed, stared at the pig and asked how it was suddenly able to talk. 'I've always been able to talk, just I can only talk when I'm spoken to. Not only are you stupid, ugly and smelly, but you are rude as well,' snorted the pig. 'This is the first time you've spoken to me. Calling *me* stupid, and here you are running around being a servant to the wickedest witch in the world, who is busy fattening you up so she can turn you into a pig too and eat you. If you don't believe me, just go upstairs and look at her now.'

Gwen crept upstairs and, to her horror, saw that lovely old Mother Nancy's little nose and chin had both grown until they met. She looked every inch the evil witch. On the bedside table, underneath a peaked hat, Gwen saw seven golden leaves. Gasping, she grabbed them and crept downstairs. She wished that the door would open so that they could escape. The door did open, but it creaked, and from upstairs Mother Nancy called out, 'Gwen is that you?' Gwen and the pig looked at each other in horror, but the door magically called out, in her voice, 'Just going for a wee, Mother Nancy,' and they crept out.

'WHERE ARE MY GOLDEN LEAVES?'

'I'm just bringing them back upstairs, Mother Nancy dear,' shouted out the broomstick in Gwen's voice, and started hopping up the stairs.

Gwen jumped on the pig's back and the pig ran as fast as he could. Unfortunately, the witch had the broomstick now and flew

in pursuit, so Gwen wished them invisible. The witch saw them disappear and dive bombed where they'd been. They easily dodged her, but she came back again and again. Then, Gwen wished that the witch would fly into the big rock, smash her brains out and die, which she did.

The pig explained that he was the boy, Llewelyn, from the farm. She wished him back into a boy, and they set off down the valley. It was morning when they arrived; as luck would have it, the whole valley was there paying their rent. They raised him on their shoulders and carried him in triumph to the farm, where Farmer Peak smiled and said he was so happy, so very happy to have his beloved nephew back.

'Oh I wish you'd tell the truth,' said Gwen.

'I am not at all happy and I'm going to kill him like I killed his parents, and I'll kill *you* too if you don't bugger off,' said Farmer Peak.

They asked him where the parents' bodies were, and he led them to a shallow grave. Then they marched him up to Magistrate Smith, who wasn't in the least bit interested, and told them it was all nonsense and to leave poor Farmer Peak alone. 'But it isn't nonsense! I *did* kill his parents, and I'll kill him as soon as they let go of me,' Farmer Peak protested. Well, even the magistrate couldn't save him then and sentenced him to be hung on the spot.

Gwen gave the leaves to her friend under the oak tree and went back to the farm with the boy. She married him as soon as they were of age and had many, many children, whose descendants still live in that valley, blessed forever more by the Fair Folk.

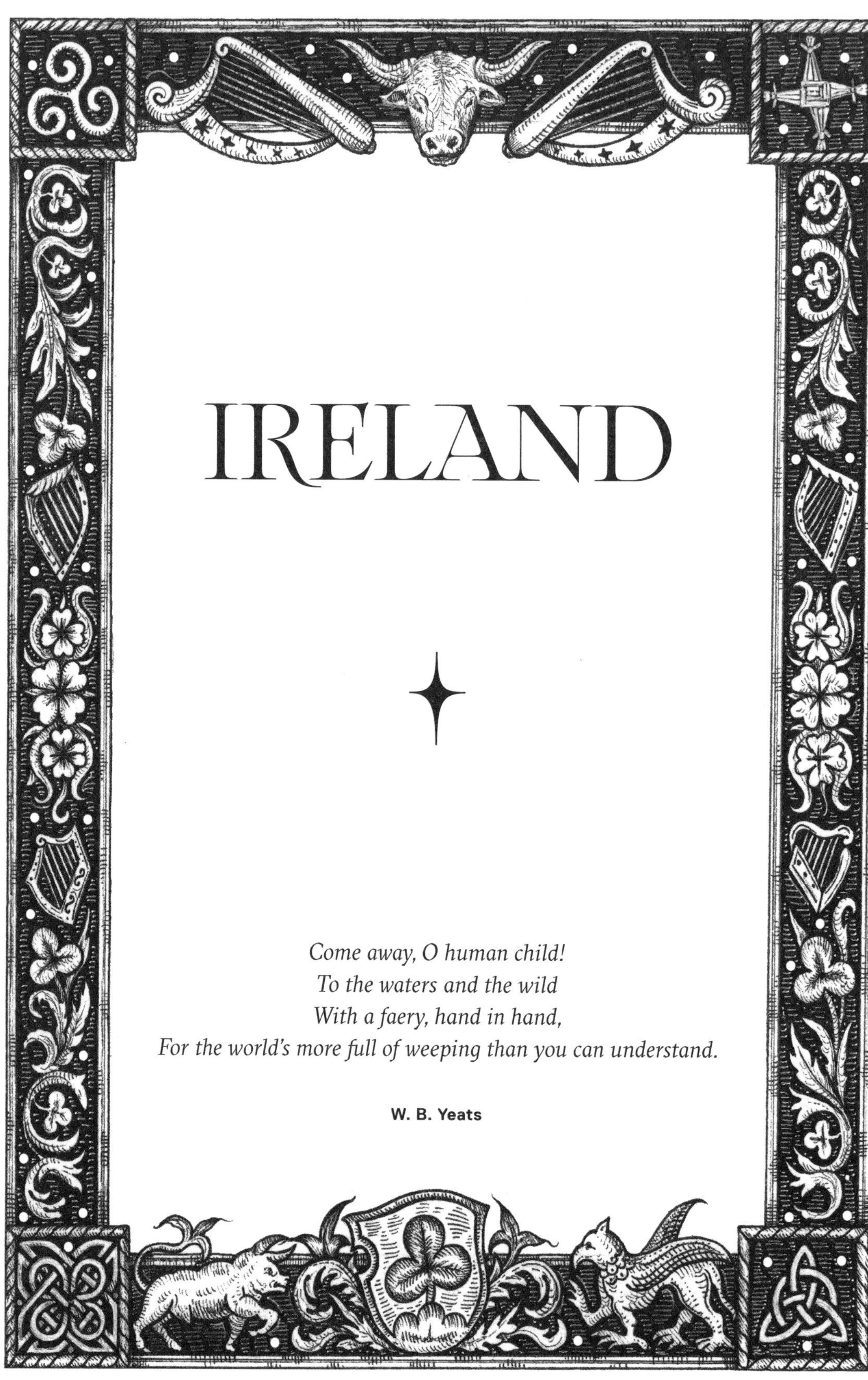

IRELAND

✦

Come away, O human child!
To the waters and the wild
With a faery, hand in hand,
For the world's more full of weeping than you can understand.

W. B. Yeats

As children, we spent a few summers in Ireland (I remember many, but my mother says it was only three). My mother had a friend, Maureen, who had married an Irishman, Francis. (Well, he thought he was Irish, though the Irish thought he was English. He certainly *sounded* English – he had been to an English public school. But as he never tired of saying, his family, the Nunns, had come to Ireland with Oliver Cromwell in 1650, been granted land and lived on it ever since, and if three hundred years didn't make you Irish, well, what did?) He was one of the last of the Protestant Ascendancy, the Anglo-Irish. They lived in an enormous – though crumbling – Georgian country house at the end of a two-mile drive through a parkland of ancient oaks. It had originally been the centre of a large estate, but in the early days of the Republic, the farmland had been bought by the Irish state and redistributed to the people who actually farmed it. Now, it was just a great crumbling pile in the middle of its demesne. The house had some forty acres of formal gardens where, in our host's childhood, twenty gardeners had worked. Now, it was an overgrown children's wonderland, for just one man came one day a week, cut the grass around the house and grumbled.

We rode ponies, cut paths through nettles and brambles and found a temple, a grotto, bridges, ponds, tree ferns and exotic plants. Francis and Maureen only had four children, but it was the children who bankrupted them – they were all sent to the same English boarding school their father had gone to, and each year, jewels, silver or a painting would go to auction to pay the fees. When Maureen had married Francis, there'd even been a house in London, but that had long gone.

When I say they had an Irish nanny it might sound rather grand, but she wasn't really a nanny: she was a woman from Clonmel who came and helped with everything. I used to help her in the kitchen, peeling potatoes. She would tell me the most amazing stories about her family, the O'Dwyers, in days gone by, and their adventures with the merrow (or mermaids) and the Good People, as fairies are called in those parts.

The story of the house today is rather sad. The children all made English friends at school and went to English universities, got very boring jobs or husbands, or both. One was a banker, one married someone in marketing and another became an accountant. So when Francis died no one wanted the house, and they even found it difficult to sell. It sold for the value of the land to a local building contractor millionaire who had constructed a big ugly house on the farm next door, took the five-hundred acres of park, and sold the house and its forty-acre garden to an American who might have visited once. I went there recently, and whilst it has a new roof, it is otherwise an empty shell. I looked in the window and even the fine solid mahogany doors and marble fireplaces had gone, all stolen. But I've digressed long enough. Back to the stories.

Viktor Wynd
at Newtown Anner,
Tipperary,
August 1984.

In which we meet Padraigh O'Dwyer and the Good People for the first (but by no means the last) time, and Paddy swears he will never go out at night again. Ever. And he means it.

Bury Me Before the Break of Dawn

ong, long ago, so long ago that no one's quite sure if it really happened or not, and far, far away in Tipperary, a poor boy called Padraigh O'Dwyer was very keen on gardening. Both his parents worked in the mill, and he turned their tiny garden into a very productive potato patch, which he expanded into the neighbouring gardens. He then rented a field and grew more potatoes, then another field where he kept chickens, got a cow, rented another field, got another cow, got a herd of cows and then another field and got pigs. His landlord was Richard de Burgh, Earl of Clanricarde, whose ancestors had come over with the Normans, been granted land and built a castle. In the eighteenth century, a great mansion had swallowed up the Norman keep. The mansion sat in the centre of its own demesne, or park, with the River Suir along one side. But despite it being perhaps the most beautiful house, in the most beautiful place in all of Ireland (a country unusually blessed with beauty), the family rarely lived in it, preferring their house in London and their sporting estate in Yorkshire. (Certainly, in some six-hundred years, not one of them had married an Irish lady, of which they were immensely proud, a thousand curses upon their long-dead bones.)

As Padraigh's success as a farmer grew, he rented more and more land. Now, with the typical profligate idiocy of the English, the earl struggled to pay for his family's indolent and extravagant lifestyle.

So every now and again, Padraigh would gently suggest that, rather than pay rent for this or that piece of worthless land or cottage with good-for-nothing tenants, he would buy it. Field by field, his land-holdings became bigger, as did his wealth. The foolish earl got into the habit of living off property sales rather than rent until, one day, he rode his horse to the edge of his park, and instead of surveying many farms and properties all paying him a modest rent – albeit one that added up – all he saw was Padraigh O'Dwyer's land. Padraigh then began to lend him money against the surety of what remained. The wise earl, realising he had to do something, invested this with the South Sea Company, becoming immensely rich, and then, just like that, immensely poor. He could not pay his debts, and Padraigh took over the house and the park. The earl took ship for Australia and was never heard of again, hopefully dying (though to be sure, by the time I am telling you this story, all the characters, good and bad, will long since be dead. All the human characters, that is).

Padraigh had no wish for an English mansion or use for a beautiful park, so he knocked the house down, using the stone to build a mill by the river, and turned the park into potato fields – another one in the eye for the English. Now, Padraigh had one child, a boy called Paddy, who grew up to be very different from his father. Where the father had never taken so much as a day off work (until his wife had forced him to go to church on Sundays), let alone been to a pub, a dance or the races, the young Paddy lived for fun, joy and good company. There was not a pub in the county where he was not well-known, not a meeting of the races he didn't attend, not a dance or a fair where he was not the life and soul of the party. People would tut, shake their heads and tell the father he was spoiling that good-for-nothing son of his, that nothing positive would come of him. But Padraigh would merely laugh and say that he had never had any fun in *his* life, and it did him good to hear of his son's exploits. Besides, Paddy was not a foolish spendthrift idiotic Englishman living beyond his means, getting into debt here and there. Why, when his son wanted to go to the races or the fair, Padraigh might give him ten, twenty or even fifty guineas, but what was that to him? His son never spent more than he had, never came to him with debts…well, okay, almost never, and those debts were small.

All went very well for a while, Padraigh getting richer and Paddy dancing more, until the dreadful day the father heard that his son had been having a bit *too* much of a good time with Mary O'Connor. Young Mary was the daughter of Padraigh's oldest and closest friend, Connor O'Connor, a grain merchant. She had good as grown up with Paddy, and it was generally understood, though hadn't been talked about, that he would marry her.

Padraigh summoned Paddy to his study, and with a face as black as a thundercloud told him that he could either marry Mary the very next day, or he could pack his bags and be gone from his life forever – and as Paddy knew, he was a man of his word. Now, as it happened, Paddy was very happy to marry Mary, but he didn't necessarily want to marry her tomorrow and he did not like being told what to do. He marched out of the house and went looking for jolly company, drink and dance. Unfortunately, what with it being a Tuesday, this proved harder than it should have been. His various favourite haunts were empty of all but the most determined drinkers, who were not the jolly, happy-go-lucky companions he needed. Disconsolately he went from one place to another until evening fell. With the moon being full, he thought of a little pub across the hill that normally had a fiddler, and set off in the dark. As luck would have it, he spied a jolly party approaching, carrying something. He didn't know who they were but that didn't matter. He could make friends and have a good time with anyone, or so he thought, so he quickened his step.

As he got closer, there was something that he didn't quite like about the party. He couldn't quite put his finger on it, but he really did not want to meet them. Looking from side to side all he could see was the bog, so he hopped into the ditch. As they got nearer, he could see that they were carrying a corpse, and he could hear that it was not the Irish that they were speaking, and it was not English. They also, with the exception of the corpse, looked rather small. The hairs on the back of his neck stood up as he realised it was the Good People. They stopped when they got to his bit of ditch. Their leader said, 'Good evening to you Paddy O'Dwyer.' 'Yes, yes a very good evening to you Paddy O'Dwyer,' echoed the crowd. 'Now won't you be getting out of that ditch now?'

Feeling rather silly, Paddy climbed out of the ditch and could see them properly. They were not quite as high as his waist, dressed in the finest leather, with faces that were not quite human, the cheek bones perhaps a bit too prominent, the ears pointed. 'You're just the man we're looking for. We have a great favour to ask. What with ourselves being rather small and all, we're finding this corpse a tiny bit heavy. Would you mind very kindly giving us a hand carrying it?'

Up to this point Paddy, who was never normally lost for words, had said nothing, but to this he burst out with a sullen shout of 'I WILL NOT.' His legs were kicked from under him, and he got a severe ticking off for his lack of manners. He was pushed face down on the ground, his arms and legs held tight. The corpse was laid on his back and the arms pushed 'round his neck, where, strangely, they tightened. 'Now get up, Paddy O'Dwyer.' He struggled to his feet with the weight of the corpse on his back. 'As punishment for your rudeness, you are going to have to bury this corpse for us. It may be that you will not be able to bury him at the first church you go to, but if he is not buried by dawn, then he will take you down with him to the place you *do not* want to go. Do you understand me, Paddy O'Dwyer? Good, now you best take him to the Church of St James and bury him under the floor.'

The Church of St James was not far, but the corpse was heavy – so heavy that, after a short time, Paddy felt like sitting down. But then he was attacked, kicked and prodded by the Good People until he was on his feet and running. He got to the churchyard gate and was relieved to realise that his companions would not be able to follow him in. Yet when he entered the church porch, he found the door locked. It was an enormous oak door, and try as he might, he could not force it.

'The key is under the mat,' came a voice from the corpse.

'You can talk then, can you?'

'Now and then.'

And the key *was* under the mat. The corpse instructed him where to find candles, matches, a crowbar and a spade, and which paving stone to raise. Paddy then began to dig a hole in the light, sandy soil, but he hadn't been digging long when the spade hit something soft. A half-rotted female corpse in well-decayed clothes leapt out of the grave and furiously told him not to bury *that corpse* next to her, so he buried her again, replaced the stone and left the church.

'Take me to the Church of St Jude,' commanded the corpse. Now, Paddy might have known the way to every ale house in the county, but he really hadn't a clue about churches. Fortunately, the corpse stuck out an arm and pointed the way. At every turning, an arm directed him. If he staggered or slowed down, Paddy felt sharp kicks from behind. As he approached the Church of St Jude he could see corpses, ghosts and ghoulies climbing out of their graves and running to the graveyard wall. When he got to the gate, they started to shake their fists and wave at him to go away.

'Take me to the Church of St Silas,' said the corpse, the arm pointing the way. The churchyard was entered through a covered lychgate, but near the gate, Paddy felt strong, invisible arms pick him up and throw him out.

'Take me to the Church of St Peter.' St Peter's was a long way away, but somehow, they managed it. As they approached, the clear moonlit sky began to fill with clouds, and the clouds too seemed to be converging on St Peter's from all around. As they got close to the churchyard the clouds began bashing into each other, causing huge thunderclaps and bolts of lightning, bolts that soon formed a solid ring of fire around the church.

'Take me to the Church of St Brigid.' Now, Paddy *had* been there, for his friend Paddy O'Flanagan (or Big Flan, as he was known in those parts) had a little still to turn potatoes into the divine Irish *aqua vitae* – potcheen – in the hill above. But it was a precious long way away and the night was getting older and older, the corpse was getting heavier and heavier and Paddy was getting tireder and tireder. Somehow, he made it to the church. There beside an ancient yew tree, he found, as he knew he would find, a freshly-dug grave. The corpse's arms relaxed, and Paddy buried him there, just as dawn began to break. He ran straight back to his father, barging into his bedroom shouting, 'I will marry Mary!' He married her that morning and never went out after dark again. As time went on, he became the richest farmer in all of Ireland. He even had a son, called Paddy, whose story I may tell you one day.

When we meet Paddy in this tale, he is very sad because he smells of fish and no one will marry him. Finally, a bride comes out of the sea and is a little bit scaly, but very beautiful – and she likes the smell of fish. Love brings him many children, but will it bring him happiness?

For the Love of a Fish

ven today, Bere Island, off the coast of County Cork, is a remote place. (I had a holiday there once with a redhead, Roisin, from Donegal – at least I would have done had she turned up, which she didn't...but that, alas, is another story for another day.) There is nothing between it and the east coast of America. The ocean crashes with all its might on the rocky coast of the western shore.

This tale takes place long, long ago and far, far away, when the community on the island was small (though no doubt larger than it is today), made up of fishermen and their families. The hero of this story, Padraigh O'Dwyer, was a sad and lonely man. For, in a small community, it is hard to find a wife if you don't have one. There were only two women on the island who could be said to be single and eligible by age. One was his sister, Niamh (who was betrothed to Fergus, who had gone to America and promised to send her the money for her ticket as soon as he had it). The other was Mad Mary – and no one would marry her (or could marry her, come to that). Even if Bere Island ever unshackled itself from the mainland and floated out to sea with just Paddy and Mad Mary on it, Paddy would still never have married her.

Paddy was enough of a fisherman to know that if he had no luck looking in one place, he should try another. But he was a shy man, and on his rare trips to the mainland, people looked at him like he was some kind of backwards monkey that smelt of fish, without a word of the English. Try as he might, he found it next to impossible to find a woman to talk to, let alone one to ask to marry him. Well, there were some women in Cork town itself he had talked to (and more than just talked to, come to that), but fool though he was, he was not fool enough to marry one of them.

On days when he was not out fishing, he would often walk to the lonely west coast of the island and sit on the rocks, and watch the great Atlantic rollers crash into the shore. Now, on the day that this story begins, he had arrived at these rocks and saw, to his surprise, a woman sitting on one, looking out to sea. He was going to shout out in greeting, but something stopped him. Something about the lady that was not entirely ladyish.

He crept ever so slowly and ever so quietly up to her. Soon enough, he saw her green hair, and the little red cap that the sea people in those parts wear so that they can breathe underwater lying by her side. I'm afraid to say he lunged for it. The creature then looked up at him with great, deep, sea-blue mournful eyes and said, 'Son of Adam, will you eat me?'

'Eat you? I'm not going to eat you. I love you. Will you marry me? What's your name?' he entreated, taking her strange, long hand in his, feeling its scaly skin and the little webs, like a duck's, between her fingers for the first time.

'If that is the case, I had best be telling my father – for he is the king under the waters in these parts. My name is Merrow,' she said, whispering to the sea, where a great shoal of tiny fish rose poking their heads out of the water, as if waiting for her command (which of course they were).

'If he is the king, perhaps he can give us a wedding present. We will need a new bed.'

'He has many oyster beds?'

'No, that won't do.'

She then spoke softly to the fish in a language he could not understand. They nodded their little heads and swam away.

They walked straight to the priest, Father Thomas, and asked him to marry them.

'I cannot marry you to that fish, Paddy O'Dwyer!'

'But she is the daughter of the king of the sea!'

'Ah well, if that is the case perhaps I can, but remember to tell him that it is the Jameson I like.'

And with that, they were married. They went back to his cottage by the sea and did what all married couples used to do on their wedding night (in the days before they were allowed to do it *before* they got married, and only got married because they'd run out of other things to do). In truth, I think it is safe to say that they were a happy couple. Baby followed baby, as was common in the days before television. Paddy hid the red cap in the wall of his fishing shed and forbid his Merrow from ever entering it – a man's shed, he said, is a sacred place.

Merrow found life to be a little lonely on the island. It is true that Niamh was kind, and in Paddy she had the best husband a woman can have (supposing that woman is not very interested in conversation or looks and likes the smell of fish, which she did). The children filled her days with happiness, misery and extreme irritation, as they are wont to do. The other women on the island did not take to her. They saw no reason to talk, let alone befriend, a fish or include her in their affairs – though they liked the children, for who could help but love these children of a beauty truly not of this earth? When they muttered that she did not keep her house like a woman should, she who had never had to keep house asked Niamh for help. Soon enough, her cottage, if not the cleanest, was by no means the dirtiest on the island (that honour fell to Mad Mary). She never went near Paddy's shed – it was forbidden her, and in those strange, faraway days, wives still did what their husbands told them to do. Well, not *all* wives maybe, and not all the time either, but Merrow did.

The problem was that Paddy did not keep his shed tidy. It was down on the beach next to the other sheds, and the other men (often with the help of their wives) kept theirs spotless. Paddy's had piles of old nets hanging outside, often with bits of sea debris stuck in them, broken lobster pots and other paraphernalia. Inside was a true mess, a delightful jumble of stuff. Paddy had never cared much for what the other people on the island thought. Perhaps that had been his problem, and he did not understand this maniacal desire for order and cleanliness. So what if his shed smelt of fish? He liked the smell of fish – he was a fisherman, and why should everything be kept neat and tidy? Besides, he could always find whatever he needed. That was more than could be said for his neighbour, our Fergus, who was forever having to go up to his cottage and fetch his wife to show him where she had hidden his things in her misguided need for tidiness. Paddy was sure this was an English disease, and he would have nothing to do with it. The cottage, he conceded, was Merrow's preserve and she should keep it as she liked.

The other wives tutted. They told Merrow that she was bringing shame on the village and, whilst you might have to listen to your husband from time to time, you don't have to pay any actual attention. You just needed to make sure he did what you wanted him to do and not take any nonsense. This went on and on until Merrow began to believe that if she were to tidy the shed, then perhaps she might make some friends.

One day when Paddy set out for Cork for a few days with a boatload of fish to sell, the other wives, led by Niamh, came up to her. In the nicest possible way they pointed out that now was the golden opportunity to tidy the shed; they would help her. It is probably fair to say that Merrow had never had such a good time on the island as she did that afternoon. They were a jolly crowd. They emptied the shed, scrubbed it, put up hooks and shelves. Whilst this was going on, Merrow saw something red peeping out from behind a plank. Tugging it, she took out a red hat that looked ever so faintly familiar. She pocketed it for later.

That evening she told her eldest, Maeve, to look after the children whilst she popped out to see her father. She ran across the island to the rocky beach, put the red hat on her head and walked into the ocean. When Paddy returned a couple of days later and saw his hut on the beach, all neat and tidy like the others, his heart sank. He ran to the cottage, where Maeve told him what had happened. Then, he ran over the island to the rocks and sat there looking out to sea. For all I know, he is sitting there still waiting for Merrow to return, because I *do* know that she never came back. Fergus sent the money for Niamh to join him, but she couldn't go; she had to look after the children.

For truly, as the ancients knew, no good ever came out of tidiness or neatness. It is all the devil's work. If God had wanted the world to be divided up, classified, put in rows, on shelves, in cupboards, in drawers, why then his world would look very different, full of sharp edges, angles, straight lines and empty spaces. Come, come with me, rise up: together we can defeat this curse of tidiness.

A truly horrible tale wherein the Good People try to corrupt our Paddy. He outwits them the first time, but can he do it again? And just what is going to happen to the most beautiful virgin in all Ireland?

The Good People, the Virgin and a Changeling at All Halloween

ong, long ago, far, far away in Tipperary, there was a widow by the name of Mrs O'Dwyer. She had one son, called Padraig, or Paddy. This Paddy was the best son a woman could have. He looked after his mother, he didn't drink, he worked hard on their potato patch and in every way he was a good man. Wherever he went people would say, 'Now there goes Paddy O'Dwyer, a good man who looks after his mother,' often with a meaningful look at another young man (and there were plenty to choose from), who might bow his head in shame – or would do if he had any conscience at all, or any love for his old mother, which he most probably did not.

Paddy felt that something was missing in his life. He wasn't sure what it was, but he was sure there was more to life than potatoes and his mother. It might be girls, but any girl he met was not interested in a boy who lived with his mother, grew potatoes and possibly smelt a bit. It might be travel, but he couldn't leave his mother.

One All Hallows' Eve, he remembered another All Hallows' Eve when his father had been alive and he had been but a child. An old lady in the village had been telling stories about how, on this very evening every year, the Good People had a great feast in the ruined castle on the other side of the hill. They hadn't believed her, and for a dare, they had gone to have a look. When they had seen the castle with all its windows lit up and heard the sounds of the strange merriments within, they had turned and fled. Many of them did not go out again at night for a long time.

Feeling fed up and with nothing to lose, he told his mother he was off to the castle and strode out up the hill through the wood. He did pause for a minute or two when he saw the windows all lit, but, shrugging his shoulders and again thinking he had nothing to lose, bold as brass, he walked up the great staircase and into the banqueting hall. He found it filled with little people, perhaps as high as his knee, perhaps as high as his thigh. Their ears were pointed and their faces were, well, a tiny bit squeezed. But they turned to him with delight and one and all they welcomed Paddy O'Dwyer – they all knew who he was – for there is nothing the Good People like more than the chance to corrupt and have fun with a truly good person. Drinks were poured; Paddy was invited to dance and had the time of his life. The music moved his legs. He seemed to float through the air, and the company was delightful. Some of the ladies were even rather pretty.

Then a hush came over the great hall. The leader came up to Paddy with an ancient, wizened crone and explained that they were now going to get the centrepiece of their feast, the most beautiful virgin in all Ireland, and might he like to come with them? Of course he would! The Good People were delighted; they were over the moon. Down the stairs they went. Coming out of the ancient doorway, Paddy saw a great semicircle of black stallions. The Good People vaulted up, four or five to a horse, but they gave Paddy his own. The horses wheeled, the riders dug their heels in and in a great rush they all took to the air. Soon they came to a great city. Paddy had never seen a city. He'd been to Clonmel but once in his life and that had been enough for him. 'It's Cork!' they yelled, but the horses flew on. A great shout of 'The Dingle!' was followed by 'Galway!', 'Sligo!', 'Belfast!' Paddy realised

they were doing a circle of the whole island of Ireland. Then a vast, mighty city appeared beneath them, so enormous and so grand that it could only be Dublin. They came to a stop in a semicircle in front of the grandest house on the grandest street of all.

The city was silent. Time seemed to have been frozen for everything else. The leaders beckoned to Paddy to follow as they mounted to a high window and opened it. In a bed was the most beautiful young lady he had ever seen in his life. She must have been nineteen or twenty, with blonde hair to her waist, breasts to her chin and all that beauty must be, but there was no time to stare. The old crone sprinkled a little liquid on her face and grabbed her. She looked like she was in a trance. Another crone put a stick into the bed, muttered some words and made gestures, at which the stick came alive and wriggled and shook, until out of it emerged a creature that was very like the virgin they had taken. *How* like Paddy was not sure, as he was pulled away from the changeling child, back to his horse, back into the air.

It is a short distance, as the horse flies, from Dublin to Tipperary. But the Good People were having so much fun passing the virgin from horse to horse and whooping with evil joy in their strange tongue, that they missed the turning. Before they knew it, they were at Cork, and then there was a great discussion and much shouting. Then they wheeled around and headed inland. One of the leaders rode up to Paddy and asked him, with a disgusting leer, if he might like a go with the young virgin. 'Yes please!' said Paddy. Nothing had ever given the Good People so much pleasure. There were great whoops and some of them even danced for joy on the backs of their flying horses. His corruption had been complete. But Paddy knew where he was now and steered his horse a little to the side to go behind a cloud. The Good People whooped even louder. Paddy doubted that anyone had ever been so excited (though the Good People's emotions shoot up and down and 'round and 'round in an instant, as he would have known if he had spent more time with them).

Paddy, however, was not, as his new friends thought, hiding behind a cloud to protect his modesty whilst doing something dastardly to the virgin. He'd seen the hill and knew they were close to home. Behind the cloud he saw his house. He dug his heels in and steered the horse for home. He had a head start. It took a while for the Good

People to see what he was up to, and then they raced after him. He leapt from his stallion, virgin in his arms, raced up the front path, but they were behind him, grabbing at his legs. He turned and put his back to the door. They tried to pull her from him, but he was too strong – and good can be (at least it is in this story) stronger than evil.

When they saw they couldn't grab her back, the aged crone splashed something in the virgin's face. She turned first into a raging biting dog but, covered in bleeding wounds as he was, Paddy did not let her go. Then she turned into a red-hot bar of iron that burnt him, but again he did not let her go. Then his mother climbed out of the window holding a book aloft. A great hush fell upon the crowd of little people and a murmuring of ''Tis The Bibble!' (as they pronounced 'Bible,' so as not to bring the Holy Spirit down upon them). They drew back and the red-hot bar of iron became the virgin again. 'Well, Paddy O'Dwyer,' said the crone, sprinkling something more upon the young lady's face. 'You may have our virgin, but you will not enjoy her. She will never speak a word again.'

Paddy's wounds might have hurt and looked like human wounds, but the light of day, with the holy book, vanished them away, for they were but fairy hurts. Mrs O'Dwyer was jolly cross with Paddy. She felt the Good People were best left alone, and what were they to do with a lady in the house? For, lady she was, Mrs O'Dwyer could tell by the beauty of her nightgown. Paddy told her not to be silly, and they dressed the virgin in the rags they had. He didn't know much about how the world worked, but felt she was his now and he was going to marry her. He marched her straight up to the priest, who smiled kindly but shook his head and explained that, as she couldn't say yes, it couldn't be done. (In his head, old Father O'Connor was not at all sure that the lady looked like she would say yes even if she could, and who was she anyway? Come to that, *what* was she?) Paddy pointed out that she couldn't say no, either, but the Father would have none of it. And what was her name – how could he marry someone to someone without a name or a voice? The whole thing was ridiculous, ridiculous.

They settled down in the cottage. The virgin helped Paddy's mother peel potatoes and tried to smile and be happy. Whenever she thought that no one could see, she cried and cried and cried, but it is hard to hide anything in a one-room cottage. Paddy and his mother had long conversations but neither knew what to do. It was not something that had happened to them before, and whilst Paddy in his field and Paddy in his house was master of all, out of his element he was confused and more than a little lost.

As day followed day followed day, a year soon passed when every day was almost the same. When All Hallows' Eve was upon them once more, Paddy announced he was going back to the castle. His mother tried to stop him; she held him, she begged him, she scolded him, but Paddy was a big boy and he just went. This time, however, he sneaked up and listened under the window. He didn't hear much for a while, but then heard his name being cursed long and loudly, a great cackle, and the crone saying that, whilst he might have the virgin, he could not enjoy her. 'And to think,' she cried, to universal laughter, 'that just *one* drop of this, our Fairy Liquid, would bring back her tongue!'

Paddy sneaked back to the wood, then turned 'round and, bold as brass, marched up the main drive to the castle, up the stairs to the banqueting hall. The Good People were delighted to see him. What did one virgin really matter? They'd have another one tonight as they always did, and he wasn't going to be invited. They'd learnt their lesson. For those who live a thousand years or more, one ruined feast is but a pimple on the side of a whale. Besides, they could have some other fun with him in the end, and then they'd never need see him again. So they danced with him; they sang and tumbled.

A hush fell on the ruined hall as the aged crone cleared her throat and asked Paddy if he'd take a glass with her. She could hardly keep back her laughter as he filled his beaker. She nudged left and right and the whole hall collapsed on the floor in a chorus of laughter. Paddy did not laugh. He smiled in a bemused sort of way, sat on the windowsill and raised the beaker to his lips, filling his mouth with the liquid. Then, quick as a flash, he vaulted over the windowsill and sprinted for home.

He had a head start. The Good People were all on the floor laughing and couldn't see out of the window anyway. They thought he'd fallen out, and laughed again. Then, one thought it would be funny to look at him lying on the ground, for perhaps he was dead.

More laughter. Climbing on each other's shoulders, the fairies looked out the window and saw Paddy sprinting away. It was too high for them to jump, so they dashed for the staircase, but got all in a jam and fell down together. By the time they were out, Paddy was half-way home, which was lucky, for when the Good People run, they *run*. They almost caught him at his garden gate, but his mother was waiting there, with Father O'Connor holding the Good Book out. Paddy dashed though the door and spat the Fairy Liquid all over the virgin's face. She slapped him hard, abused him loudly – and then, realising that she could speak, she cried for joy. She threw her arms around his neck, told him her name was Mary, she loved him and she would marry him. Father O'Connor was delighted and said he'd marry them tomorrow. But she shook her head; they had to get her father's permission first.

Mrs O'Dwyer and the priest both agreed that this was the proper thing to do, but how to do it? That was the problem. Dublin was a long way from Tipperary and Paddy had only ever been to Clonmel once, not counting his fairy voyage around the island. Eventually they decided to write a letter. After three months with no reply, with great difficulty, for they had no money (and I don't mean no money in the way people today say no money; I mean they had their cottage and their potato patch, but they had nothing else), somehow they managed to scrape a penny together to send another letter, but still there was no reply. Paddy was all for marrying immediately. No reply was as good as a yes, he said. Mary said that she loved him very much, but they *had* to get her father's blessing. She wanted to go to him. Paddy was terrified at the very thought of Dublin. They had no money. Well they could walk, she said. As she always had, and always would, she got her way.

It was a difficult journey, sleeping in barns and under hedges, getting a ride here and a ride there. In his home patch Paddy might have been ten foot tall and master of all he surveyed (apart from his mother, who made him feel three feet tall), but the further he got from home, the smaller he felt. Fortunately, Mary swelled with a confidence that he'd not seen before.

When they were in Dublin walking down its grandest street and he just wanted to run home and hide, she took him by the hand

and, bold as brass, walked up the steps of the grandest house on the street. She rang the bell whilst he muttered something about them really needing to try the tradesman's entrance. An enormous, portly, snooty man answered the door. 'Ah James,' she said to the butler, 'is my father in?' He didn't even look at her. Pressed again, he said there was no daughter of the house. Pressed further, he suggested that if they went to the tradesman's door, he was sure the cook would give them a bowl of porridge. He had just about had enough and was preparing to slam the door in their faces when her father came up the steps, back from his club. But, with typical male stupidity, he didn't look at her or recognise her either and tried to push past, deaf to her entreaties. When she finally asked if she could see her mother, he drew himself to his full height and told her very firmly she must go. They'd lost their only daughter some eighteen months ago after a short sickness, he explained, and his wife was only just beginning to get over the tragedy.

James was calling for the footmen to help him get rid of the beggars when Mary's mother came into the hall to see what the fuss was about. She looked at her daughter, recognised and embraced her. Paddy and Mary told their story and the parents realised the dying daughter they'd nursed and buried had been a changeling child. They were so happy, so very happy, that they blessed the union. Old Mrs O'Dwyer came and lived with them all, helped with all their many, many babies, and they all lived happily ever after. Good night, sweet dreams, my beauties.

ARABIA

Woe to the rash mortal who seeks to know that of which he should remain ignorant, and to undertake that which surpasseth his power!

William Beckford

I am, and I have always been, a magpie, subject to obsessions and interests that come and go. Some stay with me, like the tortoises, terrapins and turtles that I have kept since I was a boy. Some rear up and engage me totally for a while – like growing orchids or ferns – then fade into the background, ever there, but unlikely to take over. Others, like drawing or sculpting in porcelain, are always with me. And then there are the obsessions that seem to recede completely; part of myself, but a past part, like lovers who, at the time, I worshiped with all my soul and body. I remember them well, they made me who I am, but I will never call again (or, to be fair, be called). One such is the Middle East. At school I devoured history (perhaps because natural history was not an option). Brought up on a diet of G. A. Henty (does anyone read him now? I tried recently and gave up in disgust), history was where I felt at home.

Ancient and Classical European history were fascinating, but then there seemed to be this long period when the centre of the world had shifted to the Middle East. (Whilst this might have been the way I saw it then, I can't say I think enough about it now to know if I still feel the same.) Wanting to find out more, I obtained a B.A. in Middle Eastern history from London's School of Oriental and African Studies. In those days there were no tuition fees, and not only did I get a student loan but, as my parents' income was sufficiently modest, I got a grant too – and on top of that, a hardship grant.

By being very parsimonious and spending most of my time in the library (it helped that I was ill, struggling with the aftermath of glandular fever), I had enough money to buy a one-way ticket to Beirut in the first summer. I had never travelled alone or left Europe before.

Landing at 2 a.m., I took a taxi to the cheap hotel I thought I'd booked. The hotel had never heard of me but offered me a room for twenty dollars. It was 28C (82F), so I asked about air conditioning. The man laughed, pointing out the room was missing a wall where a bomb had blown open a hole, and said, 'Natural air conditioning.'

In the morning, I could see I was in one of the few standing buildings beneath the pockmarked shell of The Hilton. Syrian tanks were stationed at the end of the road, and Israeli war planes flew overhead. Beirut was expensive. I could hear gunfire at night; I was terrified. I went to a travel agent and tried to get a ticket home, but as it was beyond my means, I hitchhiked to the Kadisha Valley, stayed in a monastery for a bit, became happy, relaxed and excited, then moved on to the mighty ruins of Baalbek, where I was the only visitor, and from there to Damascus.

Damascus was the city of my dreams. I wandered down Bab Sharqi, known as the Street Called Straight in the New Testament, where Paul the Apostle stayed. I felt that, were he still alive, he would know where he was, but doubted anyone catapulted from two-thousand years ago into anywhere in modern Europe would recognise a thing (unless, I suppose, they landed in the Colosseum or Stonehenge – and then only if it was night, and empty).

I lived in a daze. The hostel was less than five dollars a night for a dorm bed, and delicious falafels were thirty-eight cents. (True, something gave me diarrhoea, but so what?) Early one evening I wandered through the endless, ancient Al-Hamidiyah Souq. Things there came not from massive factories but were made on the premises or around the corner. Food and spices were not in sealed plastic bags or tins, but loose in great and beautiful piles. I reached the walls of the Umayyad Mosque, where I'd knelt and worshipped the day before – what and why I don't know, but everyone else did. I was overwhelmed by the beauty and welcomed by the worshipers. Umayyad art and architecture remain my ideas of purity and perfection.

Beneath the walls I found a café where I felt I could afford to sit on the terrace, watch the world go by and spend a dollar fifty on mint tea and tiny, delicious pastries. I had already tried a hookah – a bubbling flavoured tobacco pipe – and not liked it. I sat and observed; I was a stranger in a strange land. The café filled with

VIKTOR
WYND
IN
PALMYRA
SYRIA
AVGVST
1996

people until there was standing room only. Intrigued, I stood up to look. An old man sat on a raised chair and was talking animatedly. My neighbour, a man with a small moustache, smiled in a friendly way and asked if I understood Arabic. Alas, I didn't. He told me it was El-Hakawati – the famous storyteller – and my new friend Hafez very generously translated for me.

I was hooked. I returned to the Al-Nofara café for the next three evenings with my diary, whilst Hafez, who was studying English literature, kindly translated and I took notes. Hafez was really very friendly – too friendly, perhaps. On the fourth evening after the storytelling, he asked if he could come back with me to my hostel room. It had always been his dream to fuck a blue-eyed boy like me, he explained. This not being *quite* what worked for me as chat-up lines go, I made my excuses and left for Palmyra. I had a long way to travel, hitchhiking eventually to Istanbul, where my parents very kindly booked a ticket home for me.

I travelled a fair bit in the Middle East in my early twenties and found more storytellers everywhere, though struggled to find such a good translator. They often told different versions of the same stories, so where I first heard the following ones, or from whom, I do not clearly recall. Some my father might even have read to me by the fire. I should also add that the stories I've heard have all been told by men to men in a traditional patriarchal society, and they can sometimes be seen to be a little bit misogynistic and racist – but they are ancient stories, and I tell them as they were told to me.

With the blood of the man who sat on his son, a genie buys three marvellous stories, in which women become cows and asses, whilst men are turned into dogs.

The Djinn and the Merchant's Blood

nce upon a time, long, long ago, so long ago that no one is quite sure if it really happened or not, far, far away in the Baghdad of Caliph al-Mu'tadid, we now make acquaintance with a wealthy merchant who has a complicated life – let us call him Rashid. To think clearly, he would mount a fine stallion from his stable and gallop out into the vastness of the desert to be alone and to ponder. For, whilst it has truly been said that no good idea came to anyone who was not out walking, all the world knows that riding is superior to walking. And therefore it must follow, as night follows day, that ideas that come to one out riding must be superior to those that come when walking. Or at least so it appeared to Rashid. (I, however, disagree. For deep thinking, I prefer walking. Riding, with the constant presence of the horse, I find too distracting for proper thought. That said, I do not have a large stable full of stallions for my delectation, so I am in no position to judge. To be fair to Rashid, it would have taken him far longer to walk out of the city to the desert than it would to ride, and it may well be that he told people he was going for a think, that he was working, when he was merely having fun on a horse.)

Rashid galloped through the desert, fierce joy and pleasure coursing through his mind as he contemplated his many deals, relationships and schemes. Crossing a dune, he came to a small patch of palm trees. It was no oasis – or if it had been an oasis, it had all but vanished – but it was hot and the shade was welcome. The horse needed a rest. Rashid fancied a snack, so he sat his great form, for he had a magnificent figure, beneath a palm tree and contemplated the horizon. In the distance he saw a sandstorm. Nothing strange in that, he thought. At least, nothing strange until he noticed that it was heading straight for him, towering into the air. There was no escape, but he trusted that the palms that had withstood so much before would see him through. The storm approached and stopped just in front of him. The sand fell in a great heap to the ground revealing an enormous, furious genie, an ifrit. The djinn, twirling a mighty sabre around his head, called down to the merchant, in a voice filled with thunder and awe:

'Stand up and prepare to die!'

In shock, Rashid stammered, shuddered, went down on his knees and begged to know how he had offended.

'You killed my son, and now you must die, an eye for an eye, a leg for a leg, a lamb for a lamb, a life for a life!'

Rashid, whilst wealthy, was a scrupulously honest and virtuous man, the sort of merchant (or businessman, as we would call him today) that you only ever meet in storybooks. He knew he had killed no one and denied the accusation, but it turned out that he had sat on the genie's son, who had been having a little snooze, young genii being notoriously small, and Rashid, as I have said, being notoriously large. But be that as it may, the child was dead.

In horror, Rashid examined the crushed remains. He tried to argue that it was an accident, that he had not meant to kill the child – but his heart wasn't in it. He knew the law and he knew he must die. He got on his knees to beg a boon. He begged to be given a year to put his many affairs in order, pay his debts, appoint guardians, say goodbye to his horses, wives, children, slaves and other dependants and swore he would return on the appointed day. This particular ifrit was already well over three-thousand years old and had every intention of living for at least another three-thousand years, so he

did not see time the way we see time. To him, a year was but a blinking of an eye. Besides, it would allow him to sharpen his blade. So, nodding, he disappeared in a cloud of dust, leaving Rashid to sadly return to Baghdad to put his affairs in order.

One year later, Rashid returned to the place where he would die, sat down mournfully and waited. Within a few minutes a furious, elderly sheikh rode up on an ass demanding to know what fool would seek to linger in such a cursed spot. 'You can smell the very djinn all around!' he yelled, but once he'd heard the story, he resolved to stay and see what would happen. Soon after, another sheikh appeared, anxiously leading a gazelle on a leash, entreating them to leave. But no sooner had he heard the tale than he announced he would stay. Perhaps a minute, or even less, after this, a third sheikh appeared with two greyhounds on leashes, shouting at them to run for he had seen a djinn. He too swore that he would wait and see.

A great sandstorm approached, and the sand fell to reveal the mighty ifrit. 'Stand up and prepare to die!' he roared, whirling his sabre around his head. The sheikh with the gazelle stood up, bowed low and begged a boon. 'Oh mighty ifrit, if I tell you the story of this gazelle, and it is truly a wondrous story, will you give me one third of this merchant's blood?'

'Ooh,' bellowed the ifrit, 'I love a good story, yes please.' He sat down, cross-legged, with an air of happy expectation on his face. The sheikh began to tell his tale.

Small Balls and the Gazelle

Know you that this gazelle is not how she appears. Her name is Miriam. She is the daughter of my father's cousin's mother's aunt's son. Our family affairs being much entwined, and being born in the same year, we were promised to each other. My father died and I lived a very sheltered life in my mother's compound. She never went out and, indeed, I hardly left. I had no male playmates. The only men I saw in our house were eunuchs. Even though we owned great farms, we never visited them, and really only knew of them as the source of endless meat, which I adore.

When we were sixteen, Miriam and I were married. I was completely ignorant of the facts of life. I had never met Miriam before, and she had never met me. *Her* father had not died: he was a brute who beat and abused his wives, concubines, servants, slaves, male, female, even the eunuchs. Miriam knew what the facts of life were and was disgusted by them. We were married and, amidst much nudging, winking and laughing, shoved into a bedroom together. She glared at me, expecting me to beat her and do the horrible things she'd seen her father do to her mother. I hadn't a clue what I was supposed to do, so I smiled nervously and said hello. Miriam was no help, so I gave her a cup of tea and we sat in the chairs and stared at each other until we were called out, amidst more laughter, for the celebrations.

My mother, and my father's other wives, had daily taught me the wisdom of women, of how women ruled the world, and as it was in our household, so I thought it was everywhere. Men, I was brought up to believe, were inferior creatures. We were but women's servants who did what we were told and were beaten, as I was, by women if we didn't. It didn't take Miriam long to work out she could be the boss, and boss she was. I don't want it to sound like she was mean to me – she was generous, told me what to do and taught me many things. In short, I obeyed and our great businesses and landholdings flourished as never before. I saw her to get my instructions and that was it. As far as I knew that was married life.

One day she summoned me to her bedroom, where I had never been, and announced she wanted a child. I thought a child was a very good idea, an excellent idea. I said we should definitely get one, maybe we should get a few? She slapped me on the face, called me a simpleton, took off all her clothes, lay on the bed and told me to get on with it. But get on with what? She spread her legs and told me to put it in there – but put what in there? She pulled off my clothes, and if I hadn't known what to do, there was a part of me that did. It was all over in a minute or less. She told me it was disgusting; I agreed. She sent me on my way.

A baby did not come after that, so she summoned me again and again. I did what I was told whilst she slapped me and laughed at me, treating me worse than a donkey. The baby *still* didn't come, and she started telling me I needed to grow an inch, that I was too small, not a real man, she said. She examined my testicles and compared them unfavourably with a passing dog's. That was the problem, she said. I had small balls. They weren't even as big as a dog's. I was four times the size of the dog, yet my balls were half his size. She took to summoning me to her room at all hours of the day, then she'd abuse me. She took to calling me Small Balls. What did I know? I'd never seen another man's equipment; I didn't know what size they should be. All I knew about the world I knew from Miriam. But I didn't like it when she called me Small Balls in front of the servants. They knew not to laugh, they were beaten enough already, but I felt they respected me less.

I was on the way to inspect some property we owned in the bazaar when I first heard some boys falling about with laughter and shouting 'Small Balls!' after me. Soon I couldn't leave the house without hearing, or thinking I heard, that dreadful phrase all around me. Whenever I heard or saw a laugh or a smile, I knew it was directed at me and my balls – even if it wasn't.

One day I was in the hammam. I would never talk about such things normally, but I was miserable. I asked a man to examine my testicles to see if they were small. He assured me they were quite normal, but how could I tell if I couldn't see anyone else's? So I gave him a gold piece. He winked at me and smiled. Then he pinched my bum (which was very odd), told me he'd show me some more. If that was my thing, he leered, he'd take me to a place where I could examine as many as I liked. He took me through a small, locked door, down a staircase and along one of those tunnels that lead to the great underground chambers that our city is so blessed with. The chamber was full of men and perhaps they all had the same problem as me, for they were all examining each other's love machines, some with their hands, some with their mouths, some with their bottoms. A couple came over and tried to examine me, but I had seen enough to know that I was *not* small. I needed to escape from that horrible place, that abode of devils, and ran out.

I was pursued into the street and brought back by a group of men. They were frightened I might tell what I had seen and wanted to kill me, so I pleaded, I begged, I told them my story. They laughed and laughed and laughed and said they'd never heard the like. They did, however, confirm, that I was doing what needed to be done for the making of babies. They had enough babies with their wives, they explained, which was why they came there for their harmless fun. They also taught me much about the world I did not know. They told me that men were the masters and women should do what they were told; well, that was never going to happen in my house. But they said if my balls were not small and my tool was not short it might be Miriam that had the problem, not I. What I should do, they advised, was test it out and see if it worked on someone else. That was the only way, they said. They also told me it should be fun, enjoyable even. This astonished me. That filthy business, fun – how could that be possible?

There was a young woman, the daughter of one of our gardeners. I got her in a shed and did what needed to be done. To be completely honest it wasn't just the one time, and I soon discovered how much fun it could be. She, the dear, knew all about it. She'd grown up on a farm. She took me there once when the stallions were servicing the mares in the great courtyard. Thereafter, she'd sometimes whinny and say, 'Let's play horses,' or dogs, or cats, depending which animals we'd seen most recently, or just 'Let's hide that sausage.' I was besotted, and her belly soon began to swell.

So I married her, and she became my number two. Miriam was furious; more furious still when our son was born. I didn't like to say anything. I don't think I crowed, but I also don't think I ever heard her call me Small Balls again. Of course I neglected her. She'd never liked me, never been nice to me. Why should I ever go to her room when I had love and fun with my new wife? Perhaps it was wrong of me, perhaps I should have paid her more attention, but I didn't.

One day, I had to travel to Basra to see to our landholdings there. It should have been a short trip, but alas, as these things so often do, it became complicated and took much longer than it should have. When, after a year or so, I eventually got home, desperate to see my son and my favourite wife, Miriam scowled at me. She said my son was dead and my servant wife had got bored of waiting, hopped over the wall and run away with a passing man on a donkey. That was what came of marrying servants, she said; good riddance to bad rubbish.

I have never, ever been so sad and miserable. I lost the will to live, to eat. It was ordained that a sacrifice needed to be made. Miriam

took me to one of our farms to choose a cow, but the cow I chose was not good enough for her. She pointed to a skinny thing, with a calf at heel, and demanded I kill it. The creature mooed plaintively and looked at me with great bleary eyes. I didn't want to kill it, but Miriam made me do it. 'Now kill the calf,' she ordered, but the calf nuzzled me. It looked me in the eye, tears rolling down its big stupid baby cow face. 'I'll kill it tomorrow,' I said, telling the herdsman to take it home with him and bring it over in the morning.

When the herdsman got it back into his compound, his daughter screamed, covered her face and shouted, 'Father, how dare you bring a strange man before me!' The herdsman was puzzled until she explained that the calf was my son. The dead cow had been my favourite wife, my number two. Miriam was a sorceress. She had bewitched them both in my absence and was trying to get me to kill them.

The herdsman came and told me the story. I went with him, and his daughter told me herself. I asked her if she could change the cow back to my son.

'Of course,' she laughed, but she had her price.

'Anything, anything at all,' I urged.

She demanded my son as a husband and half our fortune straight away. It was foolish in the extreme to let her choose and offer her *anything*; I should have offered her *something* – a hundred gold pieces, say, but I didn't and it was too late now. I wasn't at all sure that I wanted to marry my son to a witch, since it had not worked well for me, but what could I say? So I agreed. She took a bowl of water, muttered magical words and threw it over the cow, who became my son, or something very like my son. She then told me Miriam was a powerful sorceress and I needed to get her before she got me. She gave me a bowl of water and taught me a spell.

That night I crept into Miriam's room, threw the water over her, muttered the magical words and Miriam became this gazelle here. I wish I could say things ended happily, but my new daughter-in-law was not content with half my fortune, and I was terrified that she would turn me into some sort of animal (a pig was what she threatened). I snuck off with Miriam – this gazelle – and have wandered the world ever since. In Basra I met a beggar woman who claimed to have been my number two. Our son had died, and she'd run off with a man on a donkey, she said. I don't know if she was, or if that was true. I don't know if the calf was really my son, but I *do* know this gazelle is my wife Miriam. She even smells like her. Never, ever, marry a witch, never bargain with a witch, never marry your son to a witch, never have anything to do with witches.

***

The ifrit slapped his enormous thigh and cried out, 'Why, that was a truly marvellous story. You may have a third of this merchant's blood. Now stand up and prepare to die.'

'Erm, excuse me. If I tell you the story of these two greyhounds here, and if it is truly a marvellous story, will you give me one third of the merchant's blood?' asked the sheikh with two hounds.

'Gladly,' bellowed the ifrit, and sat down cross-legged with an enormous smile on his face. 'I love a good story.'

The sheikh smiled and began.

***

My Brothers Are Dogs

These two greyhounds are my brothers. Of course they were not born dogs. Our father died when we were too young, and we each inherited a thousand gold pieces. This dog here, the eldest, announced that he was going to sea to become a merchant and disappeared. My other brother – this dog – and I opened a stall in the bazaar. We made many mistakes at first, but slowly we found our way.

After a few years, a beggar stopped me in the street and asked for alms. I always give alms when I can. I believe that we who are the fortunate ones must help those who are not so fortunate. It is a sin for a man with a full belly and a pocket full of gold to pass a man on the street with an empty belly and not a coin to his name without helping. I know there are many who say that beggars are beggars because they are lazy and the rich are rich because they work hard, that one should never give to the poor, for it only encourages them. But this is not how I see it. It is the poor I see working all hours, breaking their backs, dying young, whilst the rich luxuriate and others work for them to make them rich. And why are we rich?

It is not because we work harder, quite the reverse. Nor are we smarter. No, it is the will of Allah, and we must help those who are less fortunate than us.

So I gave this beggar a coin. Not a large coin, mind, just enough to get a loaf of bread. If we were to give a whole coin to every beggar we saw, then we'd soon have none left, and why would anyone ever work for us if we gave out coins so freely? And if no one worked for us, how would we have money to give to beggars? This smelly, lousy beggar prostrated himself before me. I thought he was asking for more and was trying to leave when he grabbed me and told me to look in his face. Well, I wasn't going to look in that face. I knew what my duty was, and I'd done it. Besides, we'd killed a lamb that morning and it was waiting for me in the pot. Still, the beggar thrust his face in mine, and I recognised my long-lost brother. Of course I took him straight to the baths, had him deloused, burnt his clothes and gave him some of mine. When it came to the day of the year when my other brother – this dog here – and I did our accounts, finding that we now had three-thousand gold pieces, we resolved to give our older brother one thousand of them so it would be just the same as if he'd never been away. For what is money when you have family? Truly, sharing is caring.

The three of us spent much time together and this dog here, our elder brother, told us the tales of his travels. I soon got bored of them and went back to work, but my younger brother – this dog here – was spellbound. He announced that he was going to travel to seek his fortune. He took his thousand gold pieces out of our business and set sail. When a few years had passed and we had heard nothing from him, we assumed he'd died until, one day, a beggar caught my hand. It was the same story. My elder brother and I did our accounts and found we had three-thousand gold pieces, so we delightedly set our younger brother up in business.

All would have been fine and we would still have been there today if I hadn't listened to them. They would talk and talk and talk about their travels, of the amazing things they saw. They tried to persuade me that we should all go together. Well I'm not interested in travelling. Why would I want to see the world when I have a nice house and a nice life here? I had seen what travelling had done to them and didn't fancy it. When they talked about the different food they ate abroad, it all sounded disgusting. I like my rice and I like my beans and I like my lamb. The food they described, well, I wouldn't cross the road for it, let alone the sea. I liked all three of the wives I had then (and if it comes to it, I liked some of the servants as well). People who travel are sick in the head. It's a disease. They're not happy people, there's something wrong with them. Sensible, sane people stay at home.

We were brothers, after all, and had known each other all our lives. Even if these two were not generously endowed with brains, they were not entirely stupid. They worked out that their tales of buildings, seas, islands, strange people, revolting food and so on were not going to persuade me. But there was one thing that they knew *did* interest me and that was money. So they started looking at things in my shop, saying, 'You can get nutmeg for a tenth of that price in India.' 'Ah, pearls. Now for pearls, you need to go to Oman – they're half the price they are here.' 'Dragon blood? Why, that's Socotra. You don't need to pay for it there. Just take some sheep and you'll fill the boat.'

To begin with I dismissed this as so many travellers' tales, but I like to argue, and I like to be right. I hadn't been to these places, so I didn't know. I started to ask people who had, and they told me it was true and filled my head with stories. My brothers pointed out that they knew the way. With their knowledge and my business acumen, we would make a fortune. I didn't want to go; I didn't want to listen to them. But every night, as I put myself to sleep by mentally counting out all the gold pieces I had, I started thinking about how many more they would be if I would travel and trade. It made going to sleep very difficult, you see. I like to count individual gold pieces. Eventually I solved that problem, first by putting the gold pieces in bags of ten, then twenty, all the way to a hundred. I looked around me and the richest merchants had all travelled. My neighbour Ibn Salid returned from six years away with six boats full of merchandise and just like that became the richest man in the town. I couldn't stand this. I had never liked him. I had to go.

We sold everything we had, divorced our wives, paid our debts and counted our treasure. It turned out that my brothers had nothing and I had four-thousand gold pieces. I buried one thousand in a secret place and divided the rest between us, for we were brothers, after all. We took a ship and sailed away. Everything thrived. At each port we visited I doubled or trebled my money; I bought new things and sold them on. In one of those horrible, dirty, foreign cities full of people jabbering away in whatever nonsense passes for words in their language, a young woman caught my hand. She begged for alms. Of course I gave her some, but I looked at her and she looked at me. Beneath the dirt and grime, something called to me. I fed her, took her to a bathhouse and dressed her anew. She was just so beautiful. She said she loved me and I married her, just like that, that very day.

My brothers roared with laughter and called me a fool. They said you don't *marry* street girls, you...well, I am ashamed to say what they said they did with them. But the world had been good to me, why should I not be good to the world? She was a poor unfortunate thing, and I could make her happy. Everyone deserves the chance to be happy. Charity begins at home.

We, or perhaps I, now had three ships full of merchandise and decided to head home. Perhaps I neglected my brothers, but my wife was my all. I loved her dearly. I had spent my whole life with my brothers. My wife was new, delightful, delicious, kind, loving - and I will say something for these foreign places, for she knew how to please me in ways my previous wives did not. She said it was normal where she came from, and who was I to argue? She listened to everything I had to say, admired me, thanked me, she recognised my goodness, my skill at business, my kindness to my brothers.

We were almost home when, one night, we hit a storm. My brothers must have been plotting against us, for they took advantage of the confusion to roll me and my wife up in the carpet we were sleeping on (well, we might not have been sleeping at the time, but I don't think you really need to know about everything we did), tie a rope around it and throw us off the boat. I screamed as the carpet hit the sea and sank beneath the waves. It was my most precious possession. I had paid a fortune for it, it was the most beautiful thing I had ever seen, I was sleeping on it to keep it safe. The salt water would ruin it, make the colours run. The vendor had said it was a

magic carpet. This was obviously nonsense, a cheap trick to make me overpay, but it was the finest thing I have ever seen, and I knew I could sell it for four times what he wanted.

The carpet sank. Then a strange thing happened: it rose out of the sea and took us to a nearby island – *it was a flying carpet after all*! My wife turned out to be a genie. She was furious with my brothers. She rolled an enormous rock onto the carpet and said she was going to drop it on their ship, sink it and drown them. But that ship was filled with my cargo, so I forbade her instantly. Instead we flew home, dug up the treasure we'd left, sold the carpet and bought a very fine house. We greeted my brothers at the port as they sailed in. It was almost worth it just to see their faces. We invited them home. My wife threw a jug of water over them and turned them into these dogs. That way, I can look after them and they can't do me mischief. Their brains are more suited to dogs anyway, and they can show their love and gratitude to me.

***

'Good heavens, what a marvellous story,' cried the genie. 'You may have a third of this merchant's blood. Now stand up and prepare to die.'

As the merchant sadly stood up and bared his neck, the third sheikh called out: 'Erm, excuse me, but if I tell you the story of this ass and it is truly wonderful, may I have one third of the merchant's blood please?'

'Of course you may, nothing like a good story,' bellowed the genie, sitting down cross-legged with an air of expectant pleasure.

***

The Sheikh, the Ass and the Close Buttock Game

This ass was my wife. I'd only just married her when I came home and found her in bed playing the close buttock game with her slave (erm...that just means that they were being very nice to each other). So I grabbed a sword from the wall and was going to cut them into pieces when she threw a jug of water over me, turned me into a dog and chased me out onto the street.

I lived like a dog. Well, I *was* a dog, it was the only way I *could* live. I scrounged and scrapped over anything that I could eat. Once

I grabbed a bone from a butcher's stall, but I wasn't quick enough, and he grabbed me. He took me back to his compound where he was no doubt going to chop me up in secret and sell me as lamb. But his daughter screamed, put her veil up and furiously demanded of her father why he had brought a strange man in to see her. She too was a witch, and said she'd change me back if I agreed to marry her. As you can imagine, having been married to one witch I did not want to marry another – but what choice did I have? On our first night together she threw water over my number one and turned her into this ass. The butcher's daughter wasn't very pretty, and I don't think she was very nice. I had no desire to be turned into a dog again, so I snuck out into the night on the back of this ass, my number one, and have been wandering ever since.

***

By this stage in the story, the djinn had been snoring loudly for some time. So the four men and their animals quietly got up, walked away and lived happily ever after.

Sinbad cannot stay at home; he has to *travel. Things always go wrong. Whenever it looks like it can get no worse, it gets worse. He gets dumped by a giant bird and then dumped on by an old man.*

Sinbad the Traveller, the Giant Bird and a Lovely Old Man

ow it is time to meet Sinbad. He is immensely rich. He lives, at the time of this story, in one of the largest, grandest palaces in Fes, but like all the merchants' palaces, you wouldn't know this from the outside. However, go into the great labyrinth of the medina, go down endless twisting and turning alleys, open a deceptively small door and enter a world of courtyards, orange blossoms, fountains and jasmine. Parrots squawk, peacocks moan and beautiful slaves attend to your every whim.

Sinbad is one of the richest, if not *the* richest merchant in the city. He has agents and associates all over the known world and more wealth than he can ever spend. Yet, time and again, he leaves his life of splendour behind and goes off on his travels. Every time, all manner of awful things happen to him, but every time he comes home even richer than before, having cheated death a dozen times, a hundred times, a thousand times – still, he leaves his home and goes out into the world. Why, *why* does he do this?

***

A digression: skip the following section if you actually want to hear the story. However, if you want to read my ruminations on travelling, dreams and whether I've done a poo yet today, please read the below.

I've always been naive and assumed that what I want, what I am interested in, must be universally desired. I initially assumed that *everyone* wanted to travel, that everyone wanted to see the world – when you are young it seems that way. I am now older, and I see that most people do not want to go away, to explore, to have adventures. They might say that it's too difficult for them now, they have too many obligations: a home, a dog, a job, a husband, a cat, or even children. It's too expensive, they say, before getting into their new car and going off to see how the builders are getting on with their new bathroom. (My car has done over two-hundred-thousand miles and our bathroom has not been touched since a previous owner put it in in the 1980s.) Two or three times a year they want to go on holiday, but when they do, it's not where they are going that's important, it's where and what they are *leaving*. The weather will be different, they won't have to cook, they won't have to work, they can lie on the beach or, if that way inclined, climb a mountain. You know the sort. They're much more interested in their hotel room, their holiday let, than where they actually are. For them, a holiday is taking time off.

For me, travelling is *adding* time: two weeks in the Cote d'Ivoire, a month in New Guinea, two weeks in the Amazon rainforest (all of where I've been in the year I've spent writing this book)...this feels like another life, an extra world. Those two months away doubled the length of that year.

Travellers come in all shapes and sizes. Many are of very limited means. Some take their children, some save for a year or two, travel for a year or two, live in tiny flats, don't have a car. If they can't afford to fly, they'll hitchhike. If they can't afford a bed, they'll sleep on a beach or in a hammock. They'll find a job that takes them away. Travelling is a compulsion, like breathing. But it is a minority vocation, and few of us have had the call. Truth is, I know, a flexible concept, but I have begun to think that there is a genetic quirk, a bit of biological freakery, that means a tiny number of us *have* to travel. Clearly, if everyone needed to travel then nothing would ever get done and we would vanish as a species. But, equally clearly, if no one ever needed to see what was over the horizon, we would never have left wherever we came from.

There is another theory, that man is nomadic by nature and a traveller's need is a throwback to that genetic memory. Psychiatrists have given it a name: dromomania – the need to travel constantly. I know people like this. They live out of their bag and are always on the move.

I'd like to add a few words of caution about travellers' tales. Now, we have all been abroad and come home with lots of adventures and wonderful stories to tell. We normally find that, when we try to tell these stories, people are about as interested as when we try to tell them our dreams. In olden days, people *were* interested in travellers' tales – however, as with all stories, they had to be good. When something happens to you as a traveller – for example, when a shark came so close to the boat that you could see its fin out of the water – it is extraordinary, amazing, wonderful, wondrous! But you go home and tell the tale, especially to people who have never been in tropical waters, and they're not interested. They assume that the sea is full of sharks, that you cannot move without seeing them, so when you tell them this story, it sounds a bit like saying you went to a desert and saw some sand. To get their attention, you have to make it interesting. Before you know it, the shark has sunk the boat and ate everyone. Your audience looks sceptical. Then, you show them the proof – the jagged scar on your bottom where it bit you. They are convinced, enchanted, enraptured. Needless to say, you got that scar when you sat on a wine glass at home.

I am now only talking about stories that you tell about things that happened to you, but of course when you are travelling, you meet other people who tell you *their* stories. You must make your audience want to know more. For example, while nothing very interesting may have happened to you in Calcutta – you bought some things, you sold some things – someone you met went home with two women and woke up naked on the street in Bombay, the women having been evil djinn. It's a true story, it happened to *someone*. It didn't happen to *you*, but your audience doesn't need to know that. If you say someone else told you this story, they would think it was made up. So the traveller becomes a compendium of both his own experiences and lies, and those of the people he's met.

Sinbad was one of us: he travelled because something deep inside him compelled him to go out and see the world. And sometimes he may also have lied about it.

***

You can join Sinbad anywhere and you can leave him anywhere. His stories are circular. They have no end and no beginning. Tonight, we meet him on a boat. A mighty storm sank it and he, as was the case so many times before, was the sole survivor, cast upon a desolate rocky island. On that island he found a mysterious building, a small white dome on a pile of rocks. It had no entrance and no exit. He walked 'round and 'round it, he banged on it, called out, all to no avail. He was sure that it must have been a mosque, but the island was tiny, it was barren, not a leaf – let alone a person or a creature – was in sight.

The sky darkened. Looking up, he saw an enormous bird circling, blacking out the light. He swiftly ran and hid underneath a rock. The vast creature landed on the dome that he now realised was an egg. He sat under his rock and thought hard. There was nothing to eat on the island, nothing to drink. If he didn't leave, he would surely die. Now, as luck would have it, he found some rope washed up on the foreshore. He took this and, that night, crept under the sleeping bird and tied himself to its feet. The next morning, the bird flew off to a huge green island, swooped down and landed by a river for a drink. Sinbad untied himself and snuck away.

The island was very beautiful, covered with luscious foliage and delicious fruit. The animals had clearly not learnt to be afraid of man, so were easy to catch and eat. Once he had recovered his strength, Sinbad explored the island. Inland his way was blocked by impenetrable mountains thick with jungle, so he followed the coast until he got to a river where, to his delight, he saw an old man with withered legs sitting, smiling and waving at him. He looked just like Sinbad's father had when last Sinbad saw him. Besides, he was an old man, and it is our duty to not only help the elderly (even those who, like this one, stunk of fish), but also to listen to them and respect them. (The older *I* get, the more important I see this to be.

Sinbad did not need to be told this because his culture respected, indeed venerated, their elders, the repositories of wisdom. Sagely, they valued experience and mistrusted the new.)

Sinbad eagerly approached the elderly man, and despite having no language in common, soon made fast friends. Sinbad opened a coconut for him, and the elderly man gave Sinbad some dried fish. They sat content in each other's company for a while, and Sinbad was filled with thoughts of home and family. The old man suddenly started pointing at a mango tree on the other side of the river and gestured to his mouth. It was obvious that he wanted to eat one. Full of kind thoughts, Sinbad stood up to cross the river. The old man managed to make it very clear that he would like to come too, and as his legs no longer worked, Sinbad lifted the old man's slight frame onto his shoulders and crossed the river. At the mango tree, the old man made himself very useful, passing down ripe mangos.

The old man ate and ate. This worried Sinbad, for he knew the effect of too much food, especially fruit, on an empty stomach. Then, the old man did a very curious thing, Showing extraordinary strength with his bare hands, he snapped a big branch off the tree, removed a small branch and threw the rest away. He pointed along the beach. Sinbad sighed. No good deed goes unpunished. Still, he imagined the old man wanted to go home, and Sinbad was keen to meet someone else. The old man couldn't walk and needed his help. It was possible that he had been left for a reason, but abandoning the old out in the wild on their own to starve to death is a disgusting custom. With these thoughts, he carried the old man on his shoulders along the beach.

He hadn't gone long when what he had feared might happen happened: a huge stream of revolting and extremely smelly diarrhoea came out of the old man's arse all down Sinbad's back. In astonishment, he looked up and saw the old man roaring with laughter. Clearly, thought Sinbad, the man was mad. Equally clearly, he couldn't be left on his own. He went to the sea to wash off. He tried to remove the man to wash him too, but the man wasn't having it. Coming out of the sea, he thought he'd sit down, but the old man gestured for him to keep walking, swearing at him under his breath. Sinbad continued to sit until the old man, gibbering loudly and pointing

forward, started to beat him with his stick. Mad or not, Sinbad had had enough. He tried to shake him off, but the old man's legs were like iron and tightened until he fell unconscious.

When he came to, the old man was still around his neck. Sinbad realised he was now the old man's slave. He had to go where the old man pointed, do what the old man wanted, and even then, he was frequently beaten, just for fun. There was nothing he could do, the old man was so strong. After what might have been a short time and might have been a long time – it certainly felt like a very long time – Sinbad had an idea. He left some open coconuts in the sun for a few days and, returning, could smell that they had fermented. He took one to drink, but the old man demanded it be passed up, drank it quickly and demanded the rest. Soon he was singing and laughing in his strange gibberish of a language. Soon, huge amounts of wee were coursing down Sinbad's back, but he was used to that. When he felt that the time was right, he carefully lay down. Eventually the old man stopped singing and started snoring. Gingerly, Sinbad slipped from between his legs. He looked down at the creature with hatred. The old man didn't even look human. He was covered in scales and still stank of fish. Taking a rock, Sinbad smashed the vile creature's head to smithereens.

On another journey, which I can tell you about later if you are good, Sinbad had cut the head off a snake, only for it to regrow in the night and attack him again. Not wishing this to be repeated, he built a fire and burnt the body. The smoke attracted a passing ship, which sent a boat in to have a look and rescued him from the island. When he told his tale to the captain and crew, everyone was astonished. They all knew the legend of the Old Man of the Sea who, in his dotage, had developed a liking for the land – but as his legs were useless there, he had to trick people into picking him up to become his slave until they died.

Poor Sinbad really should have stayed at home. In this terrible tale, horrible things happen to all his friends – but miraculously, yet again, he lives to make another vast fortune.

Sinbad Has Another Adventure

inbad sat in the captain's cabin telling tale after tale (all of which I could tell you if we ever get stuck on a boat together for a few months). He got to the one about cutting open an enormous shark and finding a man, just alive, inside its belly. It turned out to have been the captain's brother – for, as they both agreed, this can *never* have happened twice. Overjoyed at having a chance to thank his brother's deliverer, the captain gave Sinbad the job of supernumerary, where no doubt he would soon have been able to rebuild his fortunes.

By now they had sailed far beyond the mapped or known world to the sort of place where astute merchants could make a fortune, if they survived. They sailed into a great bay, clearly the harbour to some sort of port. They could see buildings, not spectacular ones, but they might well be able to exchange shards of worthless glass, seashells or beads for something truly valuable. Failing that, some fresh fruit and vegetables would be very welcome.

As the boat sailed into the bay, it was surrounded by hundreds of canoes filled with small and very hairy men. At least, they looked like men – not normal people, but definitely more man than monkey. They were perhaps half the usual size. They definitely used words, but what they meant no one knew. Before the sailors could stop them, they were swarming all over the boat like ants. One of them, all dressed in red, seemed to be in charge. He bowed low to the captain and said in appalling Arabic, 'Come, come see king. All come,' and gestured towards the shore. They didn't seem to have much choice. Every bit of the boat was covered in these hairy creatures and, though they were small, they were clearly strong and armed with swords. Perhaps, perhaps they were friendly. They were certainly doing a lot of smiling, but a little bit too much poking and prodding. But everyone had been in tighter straits before, or so they thought, as they allowed themselves to be put into the canoes and rowed ashore.

They followed the man in red down a grand avenue lined with brightly-coloured, heavily-scented flowers, through palm groves laden with parrots. One of the sailors smiled and said that, surely, no one that lived in a place so beautiful could be that bad. At the end of the avenue was an enormous mud wall with but one door. Bowing low, the man in red gestured them in. Sinbad was the last to enter. Turning, he saw their ship out in the bay being completely dismantled. With his heart full of dread, he followed the other sailors in.

They found themselves in a great complex of courtyards with ponds, fruit trees and exotic animals, tigers on leashes, peacocks and goats. They were ushered into a great courtyard at the end of which, on a raised dais on some sort of throne, sat a man – or a *something* – who was clearly the king. He was twice the size of the others. He only wore a snow-white loin cloth over which fell great rolls of revolting pink, naked flesh. But the worst thing was his face. It is impossible to describe anything so ugly. Suffice it to say that it must have had twice the normal complement of teeth, shaped into the most hideous grin.

All foreigners are strange on the outside. They look different to us, they speak differently, they behave differently. A nod in one place might mean yes, in another place no, and so on. To be brief, just because someone is a foreigner does not make them automatically vile. They are not worse, or better, just different. The world is a wonderous place. Diversity is to be applauded, not condemned. And our travellers, having seen more than most, knew not to judge. When you're in the shit, you eat the shit.

The king stood up and jabbered at them at length, grinning all the while. "im king. 'im say welcome. 'im say you eat with us. Now,' barked the man in red, gesturing to one of the long tables surrounded by benches. The rest of the tables soon filled up with hundreds of these hairy men. A great feast was brought out: whole roast oxen, some spit-roast pigs (to their horror), but also goats and lots of birds. The table cheered up, especially as wine was brought. They chattered eagerly and all agreed that they were being treated with special care and ceremony.

More dishes were brought out, dishes that were not being served to their hosts. Sinbad did not touch them, but his companions tucked in with glee. They began to eat as though they had never eaten before. Some used both hands to cram as much food into their mouths as possible. Others just put their whole heads in the bowls and gobbled like geese. Conversation stopped and was replaced with grunts. No one answered Sinbad or even looked at him. They were too busy eating. Their eyes were glazed, their bellies, indeed their whole bodies, were visibly swelling.

The king got down from his dais and wandered amongst them, inspecting them, poking here, feeling there. Finally he pointed to the ship's cook. Four little hairy men leapt up and grabbed him. He didn't seem to mind – or notice, come to that. They stripped him naked, neatly snapped his neck, inserted a long piece of sharpened bamboo up his bottom, banged it in until it came out of his mouth and spit roasted him over a fire. Sinbad was horrified, but his companions just ate on. They didn't stop eating even when the king ripped one of the cook's freshly-roasted legs off the body and started munching it, with an expression of great pleasure all over his hideous face.

A group of dirty, hairy men with sticks came in, poked and prodded at the gorging group, finally got them to their feet and herded them out. Sinbad hid in the middle of them. They were pushed into a barn, deep with poo-encrusted straw surrounded by pigs, goats and the odd cow. Sinbad, who had been in some pretty horrible places, felt that he had now hit rock bottom. The others didn't seem to mind, though, going straight to sleep with the other animals and snoring loudly.

In the morning they were prodded and poked out into the fields where they seemed to graze quite contentedly, only getting excited when great piles of rotting fruit, vegetables and other leftovers were brought out. Then, they would fight with the pigs to eat as much as

they could as quickly as they could. Their herdsmen had big dogs that would bark and bite any that strayed. At night, the barn was securely locked. Besides, it was well inside the great royal compound, behind the great mud wall surrounded by tigers. Once in a while the king would come and point at one of them who would be removed and led away, no doubt to be eaten. Sinbad could see no escape, no hope, no future but starvation and a sharp spike up his bottom.

One day, one of the herdsmen stared hard at Sinbad, put his fingers to his lips and winked. That night, the night of the full moon, he found Sinbad in the barn and gestured for him to follow. He took him out of the compound, clothed him, gave him a bag filled with bread and cheese and gestured with his hands to run for the hills. Sinbad needed no encouragement, and he was off. After many, many days, more dead than alive, he stumbled into a village of friendly people.

Now I have written down what happened next, how he made yet another fortune, fell in love and married the princess, who died, of how yet again he cheated death and escaped with nothing. However, my cruel editor has put a big red line through it all and says it will have to wait for volume two. But let me assure you that, not only did Sinbad return home eventually, heavily laden with pearls and rubies, he also soon set off again in search of new adventures.

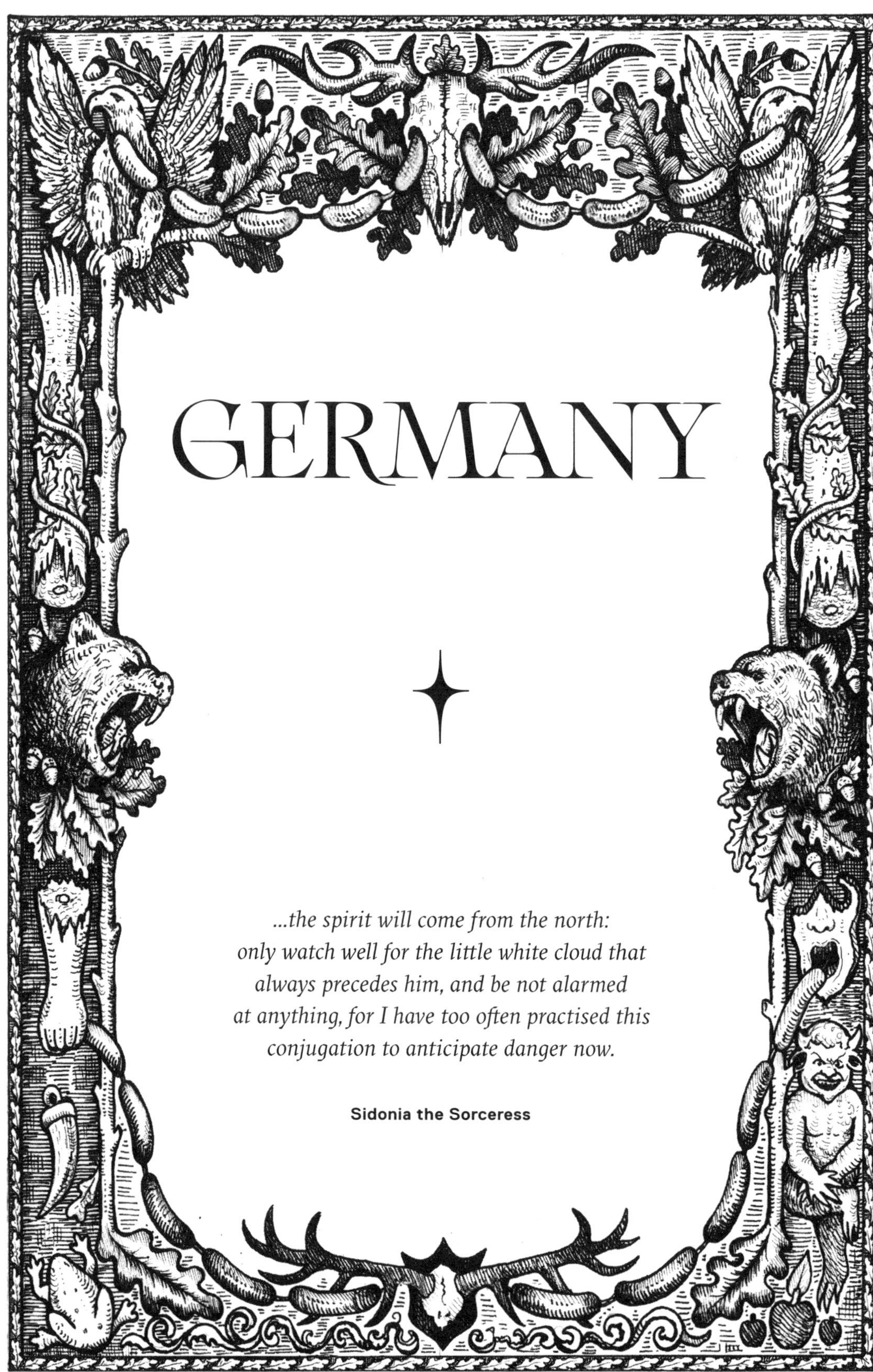

GERMANY

✦

...the spirit will come from the north:
only watch well for the little white cloud that
always precedes him, and be not alarmed
at anything, for I have too often practised this
conjugation to anticipate danger now.

Sidonia the Sorceress

When I was a student, I had a German girlfriend for a term. Well, I don't know if I should really call her a *girlfriend*. A lover, a romance perhaps, or maybe I should just call her by her name: Angela. She invited me to go skiing, but I had never skied. (I did not come from the sort of family that did ski, or Christmas'ed in the Caribbean, or holidayed abroad at all, apart from the occasional, but by no means annual, foray into France, Scotland or Ireland. I'm not sure that Wales counts, but you can't get to Ireland from Muswell Hill by car without driving through it.) So when Angela invited me to go skiing, I thought I'd give it a try. It would be good to visit a new country. But she got the dates wrong, and after we'd booked our tickets, discovered her whole family was going to be there.

As it was an old-fashioned family, we didn't even get to share a bedroom (a bed perhaps, when no one was looking). But whilst Angela seemed to enjoy the sneaky secrecy, I didn't like being woken up in the middle of the night, pleasured, then abandoned with no one to cuddle, or pushed into the cupboard for a quickie. I did like rolling in the snow with her beneath the stars, drinking hot toddies out of a thermos flask.

Skiing seemed awfully difficult and dangerous. The first day, Angela tried to teach me, but she wanted to ski and ski properly and no one, least of all her, seemed to find my inability manly. The romance was beginning to die. Meanwhile, there were all these tall, Teutonic, blond young men who were very good at skiing and drinking beer and talking loudly in German.

The only family member who didn't ski was Angela's grandmother Berthe, who was wonderful. She loved to tell stories.

Her family didn't want to listen, they'd heard them all before – but I adored them. Her heavily-accented English only added to the charm. I did get a certain amount of the family's respect and gratitude for spending my week listening to the old woman's stories. No one even for a minute suspected I was *enjoying* it, let alone taking notes.

I liked the grandmother even more than the granddaughter, but I didn't like the grandmother enough to carry on liking the granddaughter even if she'd carried on liking *me*, which she didn't. I wish Angela hadn't said that she'd really just wanted to improve her English *a l'école horizontale,* however; that was unkind. Anyway, here are some of her grandmother's stories.

Viktor Wynd
in the Bavarian
Alps, February
1997

In which the loveliest of princesses escapes her friendless childhood with the help of a snow-white stallion and a big hole in the ground.

The Princess and the Golden Ball

nce upon a time, long, long ago, so long ago that no one's quite sure if it really happened or not, there was a little kingdom far, far away, so far away that no one's quite sure if it was really there or not. It was an enchanted kingdom. Indeed, when this story takes place, the kingdom was reduced to the vast palace and its gardens entirely surrounded by a thorny, impenetrable forest. The sole inhabitants were the king, the queen, the butler, James, and the princess, Grenouille. They were all stuck in a time warp where sunny summer hours repeated themselves. Every day, the princess would take her favourite toy – a great gleaming golden ball – out into the gardens and throw it high, high into the air, watch it spinning, giggling in delight.

One morning, as she was playing her favourite game, the ball fell down a well and she started to cry and cry and cry, as only a spoilt princess can cry. She cried *so* loudly that she did not hear numerous polite enquiries as to whether her majesty would like her ball back. Eventually, however, the well itself seemed to bellow, 'Do you want you bloody ball back or not?' So she stopped crying and looked down the well, where she saw an enormous, spectacularly ugly toad all covered with warts and holding her glimmering ball. Well, of course she wanted it back. And when the toad said he'd give it back to her only if she'd promise to have him beside her for ever and ever as her constant companion, she didn't give it another thought. What was a promise, after all? 'Forever and ever' had no meaning to a silly, frivolous princess in a land where time stood still. So the promise was made. The ball floated up. With a giggle of pleasure, she threw it high, high into the air. She continued playing with it until the gong went for lunch, by which time she'd forgotten all about the horrible toad.

She climbed the terraces, went through the rose garden, up the wisteria avenue and across the lily pond, through the great doors of the palace and down endless marble corridors, past gilded rooms until she came to the great dining room. There, at one end of a table that could seat a hundred, sat the king and at the other the queen. The princess diplomatically sat in the middle. Whilst James served the soup, they had the same conversation they'd had since the enchantment began. It was an earnest discussion of golden balls and their merits, with each crowned parent interrupting the other to tell the same story they'd told a thousand million times before about *their* golden ball in *their* childhood. They were so engrossed in their conversation that they didn't hear the gentle tapping at the door until it got so loud that the king summoned James to see who it was.

'Nothing, your majesty.'

'Hmmm. Odd, very odd. Now, my dear, tell me how shiny is your ball at the moment?'

'My ball,' interrupted the queen, who in her time had been a very spoilt princess, 'was the shiniest in the kingdom when I was your age.' But the knocking got more and more insistent.

'Hmm, I think you'll find that *my* ball was bit bigger than yours, my dear.'

James again reported that no one was there. The king was a little indignant because he could hear the knocking clearly. He remembered, somewhere in the dark recesses of the fairly empty palace of his mind, that people had once come to see him and he had once had kingly duties to perform, but James was adamant that there was no one there.

'And of course *my* ball was the roundest ball in the whole kingdom when I was a little girl.'

At last they all heard an angry shout: 'Excuse me!' James returned to say, in a voice dripping with disdain, that there was a toad to see the king.

The king could not recall ever having had anything to do with toads before but supposed that they were his subjects too and that he might have a kingly duty to perform. When the toad had shared his story, the king turned to Princess Grenouille and told her very sternly that a promise was a promise. He ordered James to set a chair for Mr Toad. Of course, once Mr Toad been lifted onto the chair, he couldn't see anything, so he was then lifted onto the table and sat there saying nothing, gulping and not drinking the watercress soup, the boiled ham or the *viennoiserie* that were served to him.

After lunch, being very tired after her busy morning, the princess retired for a nap. She was just about asleep when there was a knock at the door and James brought in the toad. She was almost annoyed, but then she thought that she'd never had a friend, though she had read about them, and never had anyone to play with. So she got out of bed and tried to interest the toad in her dolls and her toy soldiers, but the toad just sat there and gulped and looked ugly. When she tried to dress it up, taking the toy soldier and its saddle off a toy horse to put on the toad, she got a glum 'No, thank you very much,' and the toad went and sat under the bed.

Well, she thought, she'd tried, and she was very tired. She got into bed and was just drifting off into a most delicious sleep when she felt something cold and slimy crawling up between her legs, heading between her thighs. She threw off the covers and saw the disgusting toad gulping up at her from her nether regions. In a fury, she grabbed the great toad and threw it as hard as she could against the wall where, to her surprise, instead of splattering, it popped. The most devilishly handsome prince emerged from the pus, a man in the prime of his life – that is to say, his late forties – with a fine frosted beard. He swept her up into his arms, whistled at the window, vaulted out with her onto the back of a white stallion and galloped off into the sunset, where I believe they may have lived happily ever after.

I should also say that the second the toad popped, the enchantment lifted. All the years tumbled together, and the princess became a beautiful woman in the prime of her life, a *real* woman with something to grab hold of, not one of those half-starved sticks.

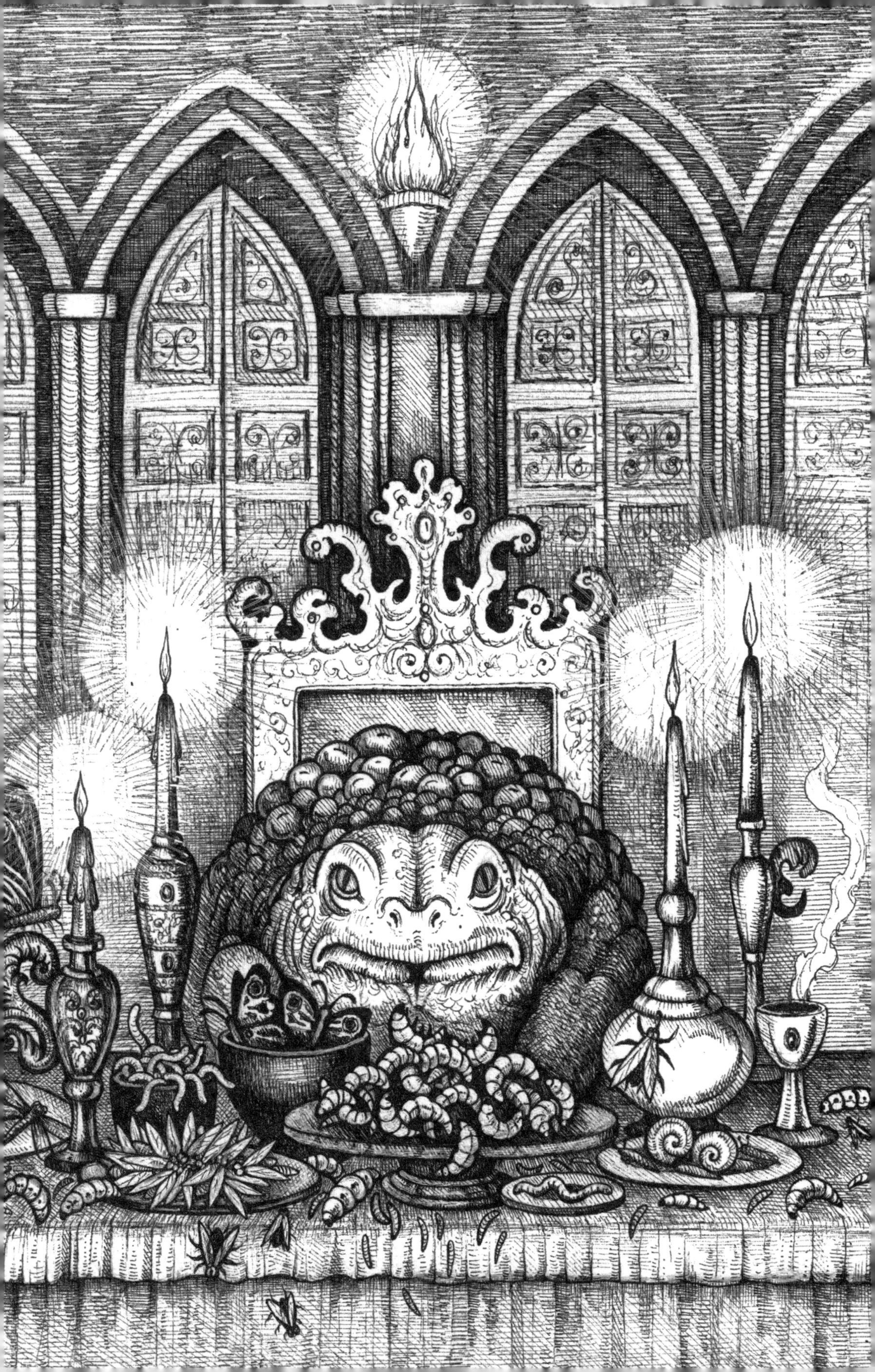

If ever there was a nastier tale, I do not know it.
If ever there was a warning to do exactly as you are told,
this is it. If ever there was a nastier magician,
I do not know him. Thank goodness for happy endings.

The Warlock, Three Beautiful Virgins and Fitcher's Bird

nce upon a time there was a wood, and in the middle of the wood was the prettiest house you can imagine. It wasn't a palace, but it was very grand and filled with the finest, most beautiful things, a veritable treasure house. The people of the neighbourhood said that it was inhabited by a warlock, a certain Herr Fitcher, and needed to be avoided. *He* was certainly very happy to avoid *them*. As is sensible and always the way in such cases, no one ever spoke of him. (Whenever you hear people accusing a neighbour of witchcraft or sorcery, you know that this is most likely to be because they covet that person's house or cow, or don't want their son marrying their daughter, or just dislike them – for everyone knows a magician's revenge can be very terrible, and in general they are best left to their own devices and treated very kindly when met.)

At the time of our story, Herr Fitcher was of a certain age, in the prime of his life – that is to say, he looked as if he was in his early fifties, with a fine frosted beard...even if perhaps he'd been looking that way for rather longer than people normally were expected to. He very much felt in need of a wife, but with a life such as his, at the age that he was, he needed, and indeed felt he *deserved*, the sort of wife who does what she's told. Since he was a collector and connoisseur of the beautiful, she would have to be exquisite. But more than that, he knew that, once he was married, there would be an ebbing and a flowing of certain powers. And whilst he was, at present, master of all, a true mistress would not be without some powers of her own. He had to take great care to marry someone who could be trusted.

Now, we all have our own little hobbies, and some of them are worse than others. Herr Fitcher's little peccadillos were truly disgusting, and to indulge them, he was always in need of a fresh supply of young girls. He designed a little test so that, if a prospective wife were to fail it, he could at least console himself with his normal pleasures. In general, he would fetch his virgins from far away and leave the locals alone. By leaving the locals alone, he made sure that they left him alone (after all, one should not poop in one's own backyard). However, he could not help noticing three beautiful girls in the local butcher's house, and as he liked his meat fresh and he liked his meat local, that was where he would go when he was hungry. He had the sort of eye that feasted on all that it saw, and it had seen these girls since they were very, very small.

When he found out that the eldest girl was about to be married, and he could tell by her smell that she was still a virgin, he knew he had to be quick. So he did what he always did: he became an aged, humble beggar with a basket, knocked at the door and asked the girl for a crust of stale bread. She could see he was old, hungry and feeble, and she knew they had more food than they could ever eat. Being a generous soul, she brought him a whole loaf and a chunk of cheese. It was yesterday's loaf but might as well be given to him as the chickens. As he thanked her he touched her, and by his touching, she become both entranced and as light as a feather (unless he was extremely strong). He popped her in his basket and scuttled off, making sure to doff his cap to the butcher in the front to allay any suspicion as he passed.

Once he got her home and got himself changed, so that he was the very picture of beauty and elegance in one of his purple velvet suits and flowery shirts, he let her out of the basket. He showed himself to be the very soul of courtesy. He bedazzled her with a tour of his treasures, his gilded rooms, showed her many curious things, including a music room where the instruments played themselves. And though perhaps he might have smelt a little, who doesn't? Besides, he danced divinely, and apologised so profusely for the way they met. Then he explained that he was looking for a wife, for his one true love. He showered her with jewels, including a necklace dripping with pearls.

Now, our heroine – and let us call her Paulina for, truth to tell, she was not very big – might well have been planning to marry another and might never have thought of Herr Fitcher as marriage material. But she was not blind to the pecuniary advantages. Who amongst us does not want to be the princess in her own fairy tale? (Perhaps she should not have remembered the story of 'Beauty and the Beast,' for fairy tales always change with the telling, and whilst nice things might happen to a character one day, nasty things might very well happen to them the next time the story is told.) Oh, and it would be remiss of me if I did not mention the food. Herr Fitcher, as has been noted, was a glutton. He had an excellent pastry chef he'd brought over from France, and Paulina was rather fond of her tiny – not to say exquisite – belly.

Once she'd got comfortable, they seemed to get on very well together and he thought she would make an excellent wife. He decided it was time for the test. He told her that he had some business to attend to elsewhere – I think he said he was going shopping for a ring, but it might have been something else – and that, as a mark of his esteem, regard and indeed, the blossoming love he felt, he was going to ask her to look after the house for him. When he was back, if all went well, they would call on her family and invite them to the wedding, in a gilded carriage no less. Paulina did *so* long to show up in a carriage and wipe her sisters' eyes. He showed her everything and explained she did not have to be worried, for a spell protected the house and everyone in it. All she had to do was to ask the staff for whatever food she wanted.

The staff were alright after their fashion, which was silence. Herr Fitcher explained he only ever employed tongueless servants, though whether they arrived without their tongues or he removed them, she didn't like to ask, and they never left their part of the house. He had a favour to beg of her: to look after his very special egg, to keep it warm in her bosom. He gave her the keys to all the rooms and walked her 'round the house so as to have no secrets between them, as they were to be wed. 'There can be no secrets between lovers,' he said. (Paulina might have nodded, but she thought this was nonsense. She had her own secrets, and they were hers alone and would not be shared.)

'Ah,' he said, as they came to the last door. 'Perhaps I spoke too soon. I find I must have one secret. You are not to go in this door I'm afraid, my dear. If you do, I'll have to kill you.' He said it with such a charming smile and jolly laugh that she laughed too, only afterwards thinking that this was rather sinister.

She had the best time when he was away. She took great delight in ordering and then eating the most elaborate patisseries. She declared, from now on, she was only ever going to eat cake. She'd had enough meat, and if she was to be kept prisoner – she was under no illusions there – then she would enjoy the gilded cage. She tried on all the jewels. One of the keys fitted the treasury. She opened a great chest and bathed naked in its golden coins, laughing as they caressed her flesh. But she knew very well they were not hers yet, so most of all, she played with the ones she'd already been given.

A funny old dressmaker came to see Paulina, a thoughtful surprise present of joy from her lover. For, though the woman (if woman she was) looked odd, she did make the most beautiful dresses, and the fittings were a constant delight. Six had to be made, she said, so when Herr Fitcher got back he could choose which one she was to be married in. The longer he was away, the more Paulina felt she would enjoy being his wife, especially if he went away often.

Time passed. She kept the egg nestled in her bosom and explored more and more, opened every cupboard and every drawer, but she left the forbidden door alone. For she had heard all the fairy tales and she knew no good would come of opening that door. Whilst she had become fond of Herr Fitcher in her way, she was mainly attracted to his wealth. Still, he was old. She was sure he was even older than he looked, and when she was a wealthy widow, the fun she would have. Besides, he danced like a god, and she loved to dance.

But alas, the longer she was there, the more curious she became. Besides, she thought if she were to be marrying this man, she needed to know all about him. Indeed, the more she thought about it, the more she felt she had a right to know what was in this room. After all, it was really her house, or would be soon enough, and once they were married there'd be some changes around here. Full of self-righteous indignation, she marched up to the top of the house until she got to the final door, no more unusual than any other. The first key was the right key. (In fact, any key would have opened it. He did not want the test to be too hard and knew that some people struggled to even open the right door with the right key when they had only one key to choose from.)

There was nothing so very scary to see, just another staircase, so up she rushed. But the sight that greeted her at the top was too much. She screamed and, her breasts tightening with shock, smashed the egg. What she saw, gentle reader, was not very nice. Indeed, there was nothing nice about it. It was a butcher's room. Slabs of fresh bloody meat were everywhere. Carcasses and dismembered carcasses surrounded her, on tables, hanging from hooks on the ceiling, stacked in racks, and tongues, lots of dismembered tongues. You'd think a butcher's daughter wouldn't mind that, but they were all pretty girls, chopped up pretty girls. She staggered back down the stairs. She tried to fix the egg, but she couldn't. She tried to leave the house, but it was enchanted and would not let her go. After a day of crying, she ordered boiled eggs and then fresh eggs. None looked quite right, but perhaps one might do.

Herr Fitcher returned, all smiles and courtesy. He asked her for the egg. With a nervous smile, she produced one from her bosom. He looked at it, and with a very charming smile, asked if she had broken *his* egg. She nodded and wondered if the small iron-bound chest he was carrying contained jewels. He didn't look angry. Perhaps things would be alright! Then he asked, again with great charm, if she'd been in the forbidden room? She nodded. 'Well, my dear,' he said mildly enough, 'as you have broken my egg and been in my

room, you must come, come with me, come into my chamber.' And smiling happily enough – for, though he had lost his bride he had gained a new toy – he led her upstairs by the hand. I won't say what he did to her in that room, in case there are children reading this (there really shouldn't be, but you never know), but suffice to say, it really wasn't very nice, and she wasn't left in once piece.

I am afraid to say that the same story panned out with the second daughter, Astrid, once she had come of age and was about to be married to Master Bun, the baker's son – for Herr Fitcher was in no hurry and had plenty of other rivers to fish in. Though perhaps she was a little cleverer than poor Paulina, for when she felt the key pulling her, drawing her upwards to the forbidden door, she made sure to first warm her bed by lying in it, then to leave the egg safely there. But when she got to the top of the stairs and saw her sister's head on a hook, she started forward before rushing out, leaving a trail of bloody footsteps behind her. She soon discovered that she could not leave the house. She tried to scrub her bloody footprints from the floor, but the blood seemed to have stained the marble and there was nothing she could do. She lay on the floor in the front hall and cried and cried and cried until Herr Fitcher found her. He said nothing, just smiled, took her by the hand and led her up the stairs.

Time passed, and it was the third daughter, Elda's, turn. Herr Fitcher was rather pleased for, where her sisters had been pretty, exceptionally pretty to be sure, Elda was something else. He had rarely seen a more beautiful girl, and he had seen more than most. But Elda was the youngest sister, and the youngest child often is by far the cleverest, as any youngest child reading this can confirm. She too secured the egg before she entered, but when she saw what she must see, she carefully walked back and locked the door. Having slept on it, she decided she must know what she must know, but went naked and wearing slippers, so she could wash off any blood and burn away the evidence. As she examined the bodies of her sisters, a strange fancy took hold. Without even knowing what she was doing or why she was doing it, she began to put the pieces in order. When she put Astrid's left arm next to her torso it seamlessly joined, but Paulina's foot refused to be knit to Astrid's shin, and in no time at all, the sisters were whole again. Paulina said, 'But what of the egg?' and Astrid asked about the footsteps. Elda smiled and gave them both slippers. She took them to her bathroom, washed them, burnt the slippers and hid the two sisters in a great linen cupboard.

I think we should give Herr Fitcher his due. He was truly looking for a wife he could love and trust, a wife who would love and trust him back, though I'm not sure, even if one could have been found for such a creature as him, that he was looking in quite the right way. When he returned, he was overjoyed and wanted the marriage consummated then and there. Elda shook her head. If they were to be married – and she did *so* long to be married to him, how happy she would be, the happiest girl in the world – then they must be married properly, and with her father's consent. What father could refuse so eligible and handsome and courteous and gentlemanly a suitor for his daughter? She told him to prepare the invitations and the house for the feast. Then, he could call at her father's house on his way to gather up his friends for the ceremony. Though, to be sure, as the wooing was a little unorthodox, the best thing to do was to take him a gift. She would fill a big basket for him with gold, trinkets, blankets and suchlike. Herr Fitcher concurred. He was so, so very happy to have found his one true love. He was blinded by love, and as his love began to flow to Elda, so too did some of his powers. But what of it? He had heard the fairy tales; he knew what true love was and he had found it.

She carefully prepared the basket, running up to him with this and that for his approval. When it was ready, she popped her sisters in and gave him his instructions. He was to walk without stopping all the way. Herr Fitcher was not so sure that he liked this new approach of hers. She seemed to be becoming a little bossy, but he was blinded by love and thought that, once they married, she must learn what was what. He drifted off into a happy daydream of conjugal bliss. He had never made love to a girl before and had been told that, where love itself was involved, no pleasure was greater. Perhaps he could get a new hobby, or his children might be his hobby. He'd always meant to build gardens. It was all very well for a bachelor to live in a house in a forest, but a family man should have a garden for his wife to grow flowers and his children to play in. He set off, his mind full of many happy, love-drenched thoughts of hydrangeas and hollyhocks. But as he walked, he found the basket rather heavy. He was going to sit down for a minute when he heard Elda calling out to hurry on, but the more he hurried, the heavier the basket seemed to be. At last, he came to the conclusion that she must have sneaked in much more gold than he'd seen. It wasn't so much that he minded the gold, he told himself, for it was going to family after all, but what could a butcher possibly want with such riches? And it was hurting his back.

Deep in the wood where he was sure he would not be seen, he thought he'd have a look. But as he sat down, he heard Elda's voice telling him to hurry, so hurry he did. It wasn't Elda's voice though; it was Paulina or Astrid. The butcher was very pleased and said he'd bless the wedding with all his heart and of course he would come. He knew how to talk to a warlock, but he also knew he'd go straight to the priest for help. Herr Fitcher hurried on to invite his friends, whilst the butcher found his long-lost daughters in the basket and heard their dreadful story. At once, they all went to the priest and the magistrate and gathered a great posse to rescue Elda.

Elda, meanwhile, got naked, climbed into a barrel of honey and rolled in a feather eiderdown she'd cut open, until she looked like some strange bird. She ran out the door and through the woods, welcoming the guests who were arriving (a strange crowd, she thought) and pointing the way. Herr Fitcher himself did not recognise her or, his heart full of love and his loins with lust, give her a second look. When she got to the posse, she led them to the house, where they could hear the celebrations were already underway. The priest took buckets of water from the well, blessing each one and pouring it around the house until it was surrounded by a circle of holy water. Then, in his great booming voice, he got the attention of the revellers and told them that those who were human and served the one true God could leave. Those that were not, must stay. Some tried to leave but could not cross the circle. The magistrate set fire to the house and Herr Fitcher, with all his evil friends, burnt and, I very much hope, died.

Suffice it to say that there had been enough gold and jewels in that basket to ensure that the butcher and his three daughters, who all married their true sweethearts, lived happily ever after.

Some people should never, ever marry. Some people should never be left alone with someone else's child. This is the story of one of those people; a story of love and loss, death, pain, cannibalism and redemption.

The Juniper Tree

nce upon a time, long, long ago, so long ago that no one's quite sure if it really happened or not, in a little valley high in the Bavarian Alps, a three-and-a-half-year-old boy called Helmut met a three-and-three-quarters-year-old girl called Clothilde, and on that day they became best friends. By the time they were five and old enough to walk the few miles between their parents' farms on their own, they were inseparable. Aged six, they watched a cart horse stallion cover a mare and were told by Clothilde's grandfather Sigismund, between laughs, that the horses were doing what *they* would do when *they* were married. Disgusted, they both solemnly swore never to marry, and were relentlessly teased about it forever more.

On Helmut's fifteenth birthday, he asked to marry Clothilde, for his own sister, Matilda, had married the year before, when at fifteen her belly had begun to swell. He was told that he was much too young: Matilda, after all, had married a man twice her age. He asked again at sixteen and at eighteen. At nineteen and a quarter when Clothilde started getting plump, they were married. (Though I will say here and now that I think it was a false alarm they both spread to speed things up. I'm sure that nothing untoward happened between them until the marriage day, and she had just eaten too much cake – for a bloody sheet was hung from their window the very next morning!) As luck would have it – and luck favours the young, the bold and the beautiful – her grandmother drank a little too much at the wedding feast, fell over and smashed her head to smithereens on the stone steps. With only three surviving children, all daughters, all married to farmers in adjoining valleys, her grandfather Sigismund needed help on the farm and the new couple were the only ones available.

They moved into the old farmhouse and farmed with joy. Never had a couple been so happy. Everyone smiled on them, and they smiled on themselves. They loved the farm, the sheep, the sound of the cowbells, the edelweiss in the high pasture and their beautiful orchard, where, in keeping with local tradition, they would make love every spring to ensure the fecundity of that year's crop.

Sigismund soon fell down the well and drowned, leaving them, aged only twenty, in sole ownership of the farm. This did not please Clothilde's aunts or cousins, and perhaps she should have paid more attention to Aunty Eva, who everyone said was a witch. Perhaps that is why what happened, happened. Or perhaps bad things *do* happen to good people, or perhaps everything happens for a reason. I don't know; it's not my place to judge, just to tell you what happened – or, to be more accurate, tell you what I was told by someone else who was told by someone else, who no doubt was also told by someone else, what happened.

Be that as it may, never has a couple been happier, a happiness, joy and pleasure only amplified, initially, by the absence of children. At an age when her contemporaries were drowning in babies and housework and harried husbands, Clothilde could work as hard as Helmut. They did not work twice as hard for twice the gain, as some might have done. They worked half as hard for twice the pleasure in the free time they gained. They were young, they did not worry, they had plenty of time.

By the time they were twenty-five they were beginning to worry, and to find their relatives increasingly annoying – especially when her father brought his great bull Herman over to service their cows. He poked Clothilde in the ribs and told her that was what *she* needed to be doing with her husband if she wanted to get in calf herself! It was a joke he'd made every year since their marriage that might have been funny once or twice – just about, possibly been *almost* funny – but had long since grown stale.

By the time they were twenty-six they were sad, miserable, bereft and hardly had the heart to even farm. They did what they had to do because they had to do it, but joy had leeched out of their lives. That snowy midwinter, as Clothilde returned from feeding the chickens, she paused, crippled with sadness under the juniper tree. As if in a dream, she felt an uncontrollable urge to cut herself, to slash her skin to shreds, to end it all there and then. She grabbed the folding knife that was always on her belt, gashed her arm open and watched the blood flowing, the beautiful red stream of life. When it splashed onto the snow, she gasped at the beauty. Looking at the tree she said, 'I wish that I might have a child with his face as white as snow and his hair as red as blood.'

The tree moved and she knew within herself that it would be so. She rushed home, found Helmut before the kitchen fire, pushed him onto the table and, breaking a dozen eggs in the process, did what they had not had the heart to do for many a moon. She rode his candle right down to its wick. With that one joyful act, happiness flooded back into their lives like an avalanche. Her belly began to swell as she knew it would. Nine months later she was brought to bed of a boy, a boy with hair as red as blood and a face as white as snow. They called him Adolf. (The name had no negative connotations then – though to be honest, plenty of Germans are called Adolf today. It always has been a common name, and all English ladies called Elizabeth are not named after the late, lamented queen. At least, this is how my German lover, Angela, explained to me that her father was called Adolf.)

Adolf was truly the apple of their eyes. They loved him and they loved each other; they loved life, they loved their farm, their house, their cows, their sheep, their chickens, their horse, their ducks, their geese, their orchard, their hay meadows, their valley. True happiness, true love, is a blessing, a gift, a rarity, a joy. But the gods will punish those they love the best. Just as Adolf reached the tender age of four, Clothilde tripped, fell down the well and drowned, just as her grandfather Sigismund had. Helmut was beside himself with grief, not least because he blamed himself for not building up the wall around the well, as he had been meaning to do ever since Sigismund's death.

What had once been, I believe it is fair to say, the happiest farm in all the world, became the saddest. Helmut, bent double with grief, carried on as he had to carry on. He loved Adolf dearly. Adolf reminded him very much of Clothilde, so much so that it was a long time before he could even look at him without crying. Everyone started to tell him that he needed a new wife, that Adolf needed a mother, but he had no interest in anything other than his own sorrow.

When a year had passed, the priest, old Father Muller, gave him a proper talking to. Not knowing what to do, Helmut agreed. He couldn't farm on his own and he couldn't bring the boy up on his own, he needed a wife. But who? Who would marry a man bent double with grief? Well, plenty actually, if I rephrase the question and ask instead, 'Who would marry a thirty-year-old handsome widower who owned the most beautiful farm in the valley?'

In normal circumstances and in a normal place, the matchmakers would have been beating a path to his door and providing a veritable parade of eligible young women for his delectation and choosing. But it just so happened that theirs was a remote valley and there weren't that many, indeed any, young women around. Those that were, were already married or spoken for. That is, all except Mary – and who would marry Mary? Not that there was anything wrong with her, as such. She was even quite pretty, especially in dusk's golden hour when the whole world is bathed in a soft, beautiful golden light. Just, well, no one wanted to marry her, that was all, and there she was. Father Muller told Helmut that Mary would make an excellent wife.

The priest knew what was wrong with Mary, for he knew what her grandfather had done with her in the haybarn from when she was a little girl until he'd fallen down the well and drowned when she was fifteen, she having grown strong pushing arms. For Father Muller had heard the grandfather's confessions every Tuesday, and every Tuesday imposed a penance and absolved him of sin. (As indeed did Father Schmidt hear Father Muller's confessions about his housekeeper every Wednesday and impose a penance and absolve him of sin, as Muller did with Schmidt and his weakness for the boys in the orphanage. Though, in Muller's defence, when babies that needed to be sent away were born in his parish, possibly even in his own home, they were not sent to Schmidt's orphanage.)

Poor Helmut was beside himself with grief and misery. His mind was not working. He didn't know what to do, but he needed a wife to help him with the farm and the boy needed a mother. What could he do? Father Muller told him Mary was a good woman and that every woman deserved to be a mother – that in saving her, he could save himself. He never should have married her, but he did. Mary was delighted to escape, happy to have a beautiful home and delighted with the boy. Her husband, well, he was brooding but he was beautiful and worked hard. As she'd never known men were capable of kindness, she wasn't expecting true love. Even half a friendly smile served to make her happy, where other women would have needed flowers, chocolates, perfume, jewellery, new clothes, silk scarves, red shoes and a pony.

To begin with, all went well. She did her best, baked pies, kept house, played with the little boy and turned up proudly to church every Sunday. She tried so hard, oh so very hard to be good.

SHE WANTED TO BE A GOOD WOMAN.

Mary listened to Father Muller. At first, she did not believe him, did not think it was possible that the revolting, disgusting, painful act could be pleasurable. But Father Muller explained that, once blessed by God, it became a Holy Sacrament, full of joy and pleasure, a gift from the Almighty. The idea slunk in. One night she discovered it was true, and from that day forth her desire had no bounds. Even Helmut almost seemed to wake up from his sad slumber as she pursued him across the fields, pounced on him from low-lying trees, pushed him onto the table and got down on her hands and knees in front of the fire. Soon, her belly began to swell. The three of them were excited, happy almost, as they rubbed it, watched it and talked of nothing else.

Then the baby was born, a beautiful girl they christened Heidi. But the birth had been difficult, long and painful; the midwife said another would kill her. However, one, *this* one was a treasure, a golden gift. Mary had never known love and, never having known love, her own supply was small, and it all went to Heidi. I'm sure Mary always meant to be good, always wanted to be good, but some people can't help it. *Some people are born to be bad.*

It started, as it so often does, in the church. Mary did not pay attention to the service or the sermon, and I'm sure if she had, none of what follows would have happened. Instead, she kept her eyes on her girl. The little imp high above the arch noticed. Everyone thought the imp was made of stone – everyone, that is, but the imp. The imp saw all, and the imp got to work, slowly but surely, as it had so often done before; just as the apple tree planted on barren ground will bake no pies, no evil can grow where spit does not settle.

He took a little time, this imp. (And yes, he was a male imp, and I know imps are normally supposed to be girls, but not this one. And let me tell you imps can be boys *and* girls – probably not at the same time, but I see no reason why an imp should not be a boy on a Woden's Day, a girl on a Thor's Day and yet be boy again the following Tyr's Day. But I digress.) The imp took to climbing down from his perch above the arch and sitting on Mary's shoulder. He started by whispering sweet nothings into her ear. He praised the boy, admired the husband, complimented her dress, her hair, her clear complexion and he *loved* the girl. Little by little, month by month, he focused on the girl, for it was such a beautiful girl, more beautiful than any other. Such dimples, such hair, blue eyes you could drown in, such intelligence, so unlike every other child he had ever seen.

Then one Sunday, he sighed. 'What a shame,' he said, 'that Heidi will get nothing and go and be a servant girl somewhere, especially when that ugly, redhaired snowflake will end up with such a beautiful farm.' Mary started. She didn't understand – what did he mean?

'Well,' explained the imp, 'that farm belonged to the boy's mother's grandfather. There is none of your blood or your husband's blood in that land or in that house. So don't you see that, as night must follow day, that farm and that land must stay in that blood? And that poor girl, poor little Heidi, will get nothing. Why, if Helmut were to die tomorrow – and that could happen easily enough – I expect his dead wife's relatives would come running, chase you and Heidi off the farm and install themselves as that good-for-nothing child's guardians, and then where would you be? Where would Heidi be? You'd have to be a servant and you know what happens to servants and their daughters, don't you?'

Mary knew all too well. When new servant girls had arrived at their farm when she was growing up, her grandfather had often left her alone for a little, until they ran away or died. This was nonsense, of course. Not the servant girl bit, but the inheritance bit. However, the imp was a skilled purveyor of nonsense, a liar, a storyteller, and what did poor Mary know of land laws and inheritance?

From that day forth Mary's life changed. Where, before, she had still tried to do the right thing, now she found her life poisoned by worry, envy and hatred. (Though at least she did nag and nag and nag Helmut until he finally raised the wall around the well, making it less likely that he might follow his grandfather and wife down that gaping hole to his death.) The imp had now moved out of the church and into the farmhouse. He sat on Mary's shoulder at all times and talked of all things. He was not bad company. He told her jokes that made her wet herself – jokes like:

'What did the snail say riding on the back of a tortoise?'
'Weeeeeeeeeee!'

And

'What happened to the old woman who slept with her teeth under the pillow?'
'The fairies took them.'

And

'What's green, screams and sounds like a carrot?'
'A parrot.'

And

'What do you call a fly with no legs?'
'A walk.'

And

'What do you call a deer with no eyes?'
'No eye deer.'

And

'What do you call a deer with no eyes and no legs?'
'Still no eye deer.'

No one noticed, no one seemed to see. They did notice that Mary wasn't interested in them anymore and spent all her time furtively muttering to herself. They thought she was going mad. Some suspected that she had always been mad.

Day by day, the imp poured poison into her ear. She could not even look at Adolf anymore. She made no more pies. She could barely bring herself to talk to her husband. She slept in a separate bed with Heidi and worried day and night.

When the apple harvest came and Heidi was, I think, around three-and-half years old...(Well, let me work it out: the priest started telling Mary about the Holy Sacrament and delights of copulation in January. She finally believed him in March, was pregnant in April and gave birth on the tenth of January. The apples blossomed in May and the harvest started on the twenty-eighth of September and this happened on the first of October, so Heidi would have been three years, eight months and twenty-one days old exactly. I don't know why this matters and I haven't just written 'almost four,' or just said she was young, but I'm trying to be as accurate as possible and not leave anything out. Sorry where was I? Ah yes.) When the apple harvest came and Heidi was three years, eight months and twenty-one days old, the imp decided it was time to act.

'Just look at the boy running around underneath the apple trees, as though he's a little lord, as if it all belongs to him.'

'But it does!' Mary sobbed in reply. 'It does, or good as does.'

As if by magic, Helmut fell off his ladder (as indeed it was magic, if you can call an imp leaping at the speed of lightning off a lady's shoulder, giving a ladder a good push and returning to the shoulder before anyone noticed he was gone 'magic'). Mary ran to pick up Helmut. He was fine, not even a tiny bit hurt, definitely not dead. 'But he could be dead next time,' murmured the imp, 'and then where would you be? They'd send you off on your ear and put your little girl in Father Schmidt's orphanage, and you know what happens to little girls there?' (Not much actually. Father Schmidt only liked boys, and not for much longer. One of them, Wilhelm, helped along by a brother imp, was just setting fire to the curtains around the bed where Father Schmidt lay sleeping and soon burnt to a crisp. Imps aren't always bad, you see. In fact, I'm not at all sure that they are good or bad, they're just imps. They do what imps always have done, always will do. Sometimes we approve and sometimes we disapprove, but ultimately, we are all unwitting actors in a play put on just for their amusement. Today, I suspect, we all approve of Wilhelm's actions, but not then. The judge sentenced him to hang. He knew all about Father Schmidt – he who was a generous benefactor to the orphanage, which came with terrible advantages. The judge was furious – he did not like the look of Father Schmidt's replacement, Father Heinrich. He thought he'd lost his Tuesday treat – though, as it happens, Heinrich was just holding out for more money. Which of course he got, but that is another story.)

'But what can I do?' demanded Mary.

'As to that, it is very simple,' replied the imp. 'You must kill the boy and then Heidi will get everything.'

'But how?'

'Ah, but that too is very simple.'

The imp – let's call him Charles – told her to wait until the cart was loaded up with apples and Helmut had gone to market. 'Now's your chance. *Kill the boy*! Get him to help you taking apples up to the apple press.'

The great metal-lined chest was where they stored their own supply, often right through to August. Once there, Adolf started arranging the apples. 'Now! Now's your chance, slam the lid down.' So she slammed the lid down and it cut the boy's head off neatly at the neck. She opened the chest, picked up the head, looked at the dead face and laughed. She laughed and laughed and laughed. She thought her pants would never dry. Heidi was safe now, no orphanage for her. The house was hers, the farm was hers, hurray. But a little doubt crept uninvited into her head – what would her husband say? What should she do? What could she do with the body?

As though he could read her thoughts (which of course he could), Charles whispered instructions. She was to take the body to the house, put it sitting up on a chair before the fire, balance the head on the neck and wrap a scarf around the wound. 'Now go, find Heidi, tell her to fetch the boy.'

Heidi returned. 'He doesn't answer, Mama.'

'Oh what a naughty, wicked, good-for-nothing child he is! You

go back and punch him on the ear, that'll learn him.'

'Mummy, Mummy, his head has fallen off!'

'Oh no, you've killed your brother! Never mind dear, such things happen all the time. Like that time last week when Adolf spilt the milk.'

Heidi cried, for Adolf had been soundly thrashed by his father for knocking over the milk churn, and she did not want a thrashing – 'But never, ever tell your father or he'll thrash you too,' Mary said. Gentle reader, do not forget that Heidi was not yet four years old and knew nothing of the world. For all she knew, it was normal to kill your own brother.

'But what shall I do with the body?' Mary asked the imp.

'Nothing simpler: make him into sausages,' Charles replied.

She made young Adolf into sausages and gave the bones to Heidi to bury beneath the juniper tree. Helmut came back from market and asked about the boy, since Adolf normally ran to meet him and hugged him tight, all the tighter since Mary had stopped even trying or pretending to love him.

'Oh,' said Mary, 'Erm. Well...,' and prompted by the imp, explained how the boy's uncle had come and taken him off to work on his distant farm. Helmut thought this was a bit odd, but then his nose picked up the most delicious aroma it had ever smelt. 'I smell sausages!' he yelled. He rushed into the kitchen, where he proceeded to eat and eat and eat until he had finished the sausages.

'What a disgusting man,' Charles whispered to Mary. 'He's eaten his own son. You'll have to kill him too, you know.'

Just as Helmut finished the sausages, over the mountain in the nearby town a beautiful bird appeared, a red bird with white wings. It settled in a tree outside the town jeweller Hans's shop and sang a song so beautiful that Hans came out with tears in his eyes and put a thick golden chain around the bird's neck. The bird then flew to the tree outside the cobbler's shop and sang his song so beautifully that the cobbler came out and put a fine pair of leather boots around his neck. The bird then went to the tree outside the mill and sang his beautiful song. The millers stopped their milling and came out to listen. With tears in their eyes they put a millstone around the bird's neck. He flew over the mountain and settled in the juniper tree outside Helmut's farmhouse.

Inside, they stopped their squabbling and listened to the bird's song. It was the most beautiful song that Helmut and Heidi had ever heard. But it was the most hideous song that Mary had ever heard, for she heard the words behind the music, and the words the bird sang were:

My mother she killed me
My father he ate me
My sister she buried me

Over and over, again and again. It drove Mary mad – not that Helmut thought that would be a long drive. She screamed, begging them not to go out. As Mary held onto Helmut, who was now convinced that she was mad, Heidi crept out and went to see the bird. It dropped the golden chain around her neck, and she ran into the house, screaming with joy. Helmut went out and came back with the boots. Then, yelling with fear, urged on she knew not how, Mary went out, and the bird sang:

My mother she killed me
My father he ate me
My sister she buried me

Then the bird dropped the millstone onto her head, smashing it into a thousand little pieces. Helmut married the pretty young woman next door and had six more daughters who all, like Heidi, married well. And they all lived happily ever after.

NORWAY

✦

Be merciful. You do not understand me;
I live in the woods by choice – that is my happiness.
Here, where I am all alone, it can hurt no one
that I am as I am; but when I go among others, I have
to use all my will power to be as I should.

Knut Hamsun

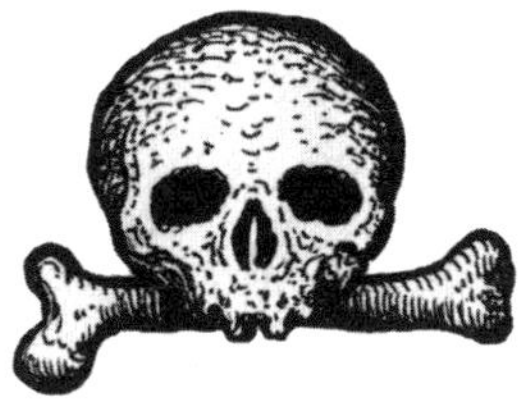

Norway is a beautiful country full of beautiful people but, like much of Scandinavia, is sparsely populated. Everyone grows up knowing everyone else, and there seems to come a time when almost all of the boys and girls think they should head south in search of fun. Of course, us southerners welcome these northern adventurers with outstretched arms and unmade beds, so whilst the population of Scandinavia is rather small, at one time or other, almost the entire world has had a Scandinavian lover. (Unfortunately for us, when it comes to actually settling down and marrying, Scandinavians tend to prefer their childhood sweetheart or someone they grew up with and never realised they fancied, never realised that he or she or they were so very, very pretty, until they'd had a good look around abroad. So they go back home leaving a trail of broken hearts behind them – for, whilst for them we were but a holiday romance, for us they were and will always be The One, every single one of them.)

Perhaps it is no surprise, then, that I too, in my twenties, had a Swedish girlfriend, Malin, who was rather lovely and loving. Her uncle was married to a Norwegian and had a summer cabin on a fjord. I have rarely been anywhere so beautiful. The mountains crashed into the waves, the cabin was perched on a rock, fish jumped out of the sea longing to be caught. However, whilst my girlfriend was wonderful in every way, at the time, it was tricky being on holiday with a group of foreigners who liked to drink and sing late into the night. Though they could all speak English, and indeed did some of the time, they were more likely to speak Norwegian amongst themselves. So if I did not constantly make myself the centre of attention, I was left out.

Sensing my boredom, Malin borrowed her uncle's flat in Oslo and off we went. The first thing we saw at the train station was a poster for an annual storytelling festival. Norwegian isn't that different from Swedish, and now having been in the country for three weeks, I understood it pretty well. At the festival, I discovered the world of Norwegian fairy tales – a place full of thoroughly unpleasant trolls that enjoy eating people.

Back home in London, we went a few times to hear storytellers sponsored by the Norwegian embassy. I was in love, truly, deeply, forever in love. Malin, however, was a little bored. She went home for a couple of weeks before planning to come to my parents' for Christmas. Then she said she'd really missed her parents and her grandfather, and was going to stay for Christmas, but she'd be back for the New Year's Eve Masquerade Ball I was throwing at Covent Garden's Arts Theatre. Then, just like that, I got a text to say not to meet her at the airport on 30 December after all, as she'd been spending a lot of time with a man she'd been to school with, who now managed the local bank. He really was much more suited to her, and whilst I was very nice, she wanted a grownup, not a boy. Would I mind if they both came to the party? Well, I'd sold two-thousand tickets, so it seemed churlish to say no, but I really didn't need to stumble across them at 4 a.m. eating each other's faces out.

My heart shattered into a million tiny pieces, and I cried for six months. Her best friend didn't help much when he commiserated with typical Scandinavian stoicism, saying that the thing about women was that they were like buses, and if I went to a bus stop, another was sure to come along. Though really, my best bet was to go to Stansted Airport and greet the flights from Stockholm, full of Swedish boys and girls coming to London looking for fun. Meanwhile, Malin was pregnant and getting married. (I wish her well and thank her for the introduction to her culture.)

Viktor Wynd
and Malin
visiting
Romsdalen,
July 2003

The most beautiful princess in the world meets the most beautiful bear in the world. The ugliest troll hag in the world steals the bear for her bed. Will love save the day?

For the Love of an Ice Bear

nce upon a time, long, long ago, so long ago that time seemed to stand still, century flowed into century, one life was very like another, but everyone and everything had its place and no one expected things to change. Let me take you to a little kingdom, a tiny kingdom. In fact, I'm not even sure if the king was a king. There are, after all, only five true kings: the kings of England, Hearts, Clubs, Spades and, of course, Diamonds – but we'll call him a king for the sake of the story. He was a good king, married to a good queen, and they first had two daughters, Batilde and Brina. Perhaps it is no surprise, with names like that, meaning 'female warrior' and 'defender,' that they were both extremely ugly. However, it is dangerous to automatically confuse ugliness with meanness or badness. They were both everything a daughter and everything a princess should be in every way, apart from their lamentable looks. After a long wait a third child, also a daughter, was born. She was so beautiful, so very beautiful, that they could call her nothing but Astrilde (which means 'beauty').

Astrilde was the most beautiful baby that anyone had ever seen. I am aware that I have said this about other babies in this book, and will say it again (and indeed, have also said it about each of my babies in turn, and all of my friends' babies, but I must ask you here to believe me when I say that *she* was the most beautiful child anyone had ever seen, and all loved her). Her parents loved her, her sisters loved her, the whole court loved her. They would all do anything for one of her smiles. Like the sun spreads warmth with his gaze, she radiated joy and happiness. It would have taken great strength of character for a girl, let alone a princess, to grow up as the apple of everybody's eye and not be a little, well, we might call it spoilt. But on the whole she was a joy to all, a bright ray of light in the dark Nordic winter. And why should a princess not expect her every whim to be met? Especially when they were nearly always wholesome whims.

When she was...well, let us call her sixteen, certainly well past childhood but not yet an adult, she had a recurring dream. She dreamt of a golden wreath, but it was more than a golden wreath. It was everything, it was love, it was happiness, it was wholeness. It was also a strange pins-and-needles longing, an unfamiliar warmth inside her, a melting of her body. She awoke with the wreath vivid in her mind. It was too real to have just been a dream. Besides, in the whole of recorded human history, until it seems just yesterday, what happens in the dream-world has been considered as important, if not more important, than what happens when one is awake. In olden days few things were more interesting, more important, than dreams. Indeed, if you added up the time people spent dreaming and the time people spent discussing their dreams, dreams were more than half of peoples' lives. (Dreams are where the two worlds meet, where the veil is thinnest, where messages come and signs are seen. I will say it once, and I will say it here: we ignore dreams at our peril.)

All the wise men and magicians at her father's court heard Princess Astrilde's dream and agreed that this wreath was indeed real. Without this wreath, the princess was miserable. It was all she could talk about; all she could think about. Her happy, beautiful face no longer lit up the court's endless dark, cold winter. Instead, all muttered and all worried and all wondered: how to get this wreath for their princess. Perhaps, if she had been brought up differently, she would not have seen the world as a place that existed solely to provide her with her wants and been less dismayed when it couldn't, but I doubt it. Messengers were sent, goldsmiths summoned, and all donated the gold they had so that such a wreath could be made, but it was never the wreath of her dreams. She got thinner and sadder, and the court all cried with her.

Miserable day followed miserable day, months bled together, until the day Astrilde went galloping fearlessly on her pony across the snow and saw an ice bear. Normally when people saw ice bears they ran, but Astrilde felt strangely drawn to this bear, who, seeing her, lay down on his back and waved. She could resist no longer; she dismounted and approached.

'I've been waiting for you,' said the bear, with what certainly appeared to be a friendly smile (inasmuch as bears can smile, which they can't – but it was very like). Then, with a start, she saw that the bear was playing with a golden wreath. And not just any golden wreath, but *her* golden wreath from dreamland! Stuttering, she asked if she could have it.

'Of course you can, it is your wreath, but if I give it to you, you must promise to come with me next Woden's Day.'

Perhaps she didn't really understand what a promise was. There'd been no consequences to the many she had broken, but perhaps something else was at play. In all events, to live without the wreath was an unbearable penalty, so she promised and rode home happier than she had ever been. Her joy and happiness lit up the court. All shared smiles. All who saw her felt joy again, a joy that had gone out of their world when she had started the golden dreams. A great weight had been lifted off the kingdom.

However, none knew what to make of the tale of the great white bear. It seemed so unlikely and so lightly told. Ice bears never came near the town, and besides, how could such a wreath be made by those great clumsy paws? That bears could talk, none disputed.

Come Woden's Day, the ice bear was seen, and the guards ran out. It was a mighty bear, and as it roared they all ran away, bar one who stood firm, but his spear bounced off the bear and he was killed. The bear sat beneath the royal hall and roared. None dared go and fight it. All trembled with fear, until the warrior princess Batilde said that she could not bear to see her darling sister sacrificed to a great ice bear and she would go in her place. Down went Batilde. She mounted the bear's back and disappeared from sight as it galloped into the snow. They hadn't gone far when the bear stopped, gently put her down, drew back her veil with a paw and then roared in anger, 'You are not the one, you are old and ugly, so *very* ugly!' and chased her home.

When Woden's Day came around again, they were ready for the bear. The folk were armed. A great fire burnt in the courtyard of the King's Hall. All knew bears feared fire, but still the bear came. Ten men stood firm and ten were killed. Then, the bear sauntered through the fire, but fire itself was afraid of this bear and, not daring to burn him, went out. The bear sat before the double doors of the King's Hall and roared. All inside quaked with fear. The king, who had sworn that if the bear came back he would fight it to the death rather than surrender his daughter, was silent. All looked at him and again, the bear roared. The defender princess, Brina, spoke up to say it was better that she go and be killed by the dreadful bear than her poor beautiful sister. Astrilde was the only one who was not afraid and muttered something about the bear being a very nice bear and having other things on his mind than death. But no one listened to her, for she was but a girl. Brina went down, mounted the bear's back and disappeared with him into the snowy forested mountains. There, he put her down, drew back her veil with a paw and roared in anger, 'You are not the one, you are ugly, so very *ugly*, you look like a cat's bottom, not a princess!' and chased her home.

On the third Woden's Day as all the court wept, the princess Astrilde traipsed merrily down the steps. Grasping her wreath, she leapt onto the bear's back and vanished into the snow, the ice and the great endless forest. They hadn't gone far when the bear gently set her down, removed her veil and stroked her face with his mighty paw. Then his nose nuzzled her nose. Their eyes met and then their tongues. She felt herself gripped in his mighty embrace and felt her body, as if it knew it was home, embrace him back. The kisses went on and on until the bear laid her gently down on the snow and, to the sound of mutual joy and ecstatic cries, took her maidenhead. Then soon, too soon, oh *far* too soon he put her on his back, and they were away again, galloping due north. But it wasn't long before he again felt the need to look at her and she felt the need to look back, and their tongues and their bodies the need to meet and form one thing, half bear, half princess (well more like 90 per cent bear). This way, the journey north was frequently broken, for there were no missionaries then in the frozen north to teach girls what was and was not a sin or what position was and was not allowed. And then the bear was lying on his back in the snow, and she was riding his flagpole like she had never ridden anything before. It is to be doubted if ever greater joy, happiness or pleasure had been felt by anyone ever as was felt by her when the great bear exploded inside her in a great avalanche of ecstasy.*

Long and far was the journey, and farther than far. They came to a great castle, empty and cold, until they finally happened upon a chamber where a fire burnt. The bear put her down and served the wedding feast.

Here she lived with her bear, her love, who was mostly there, except when he was gone. And he was never gone for long, a week at most perhaps, a week that passed quickly with dreams of her bear. Sometimes on moonless nights, as they made love on their great four-poster bed, she felt his great hairy bear body transform into a man – and what a man, beautiful, soft, giving flesh, her dream of all that was manly and desirable. None of those nasty, tight muscles of labourers and immature young men, no flat tummy he, but a *proper* man, a man with lumps and a man to love, *a real man*. She could only dream of the glory his bearded face must be.

She soon had a child, but the bear took it. She was sad, but she loved her bear. It was when the second baby was taken that the dreams began, dreams of home. Who put them there and how they got there we can only guess, but dreams come from somewhere, from someone, from something, and always have an aim, sometimes good but sometimes bad. Someone else wanted that bear, and that someone

* Norwegians have a somewhat undeserved reputation for dourness. I have heard this tale told on several occasions, and when children are present, the bear is merely a loveably cuddly polar bear, but generally much is made of their honeymoon. Indeed, one evening, after a fair amount of vodka had been drunk, my girlfriend's aunt told the tale, and told it to make me blush, for there was very little in her version that was *not* about the physical aspects of bear/princess loving. Much was made of some word play. Malin's brother (who, to be honest, I don't think liked me) told me that the Norwegian word for 'ice bear' ('isbjorn') and the Norwegian for penis ('bokmal'), when pronounced in a certain regional accent, sound very alike – and this is without taking into account that many Norwegian men call their manhoods 'lille bjorn' ('little bear') when sleeping, and 'stor bjorn' ('great bear') when they are standing proud. In my retelling, I have tried to stay as close to the original as possible but have felt the need to slightly tone down the erotic elements. Perhaps that version is for a more specialised publication, and indeed, a specialised teller.

else was fighting for him in dreamland. After the bear's theft of her third child, these dreams took over. Astrilde became miserable. She begged and pleaded to be allowed home, just for one week, to embrace her parents and her loving, hideous sisters, such dear creatures. Even if they did look like cats' bottoms, they were her sisters and she loved them, she wanted to see them. The princess in her had always got her way, so despite the bear's entreaties, she insisted.

Finally, the great bear could resist no longer. Who amongst us could? He agreed to take her home for a week on the condition that she promise she would listen to her father but not her mother. She promised, jumped on his back and they raced through the frozen forests, across the ice and snow to her father's land.

All in her father's hall were overjoyed to see her again. Some had listened to the court warlock who'd said he'd seen no evil in the bear, and that all could see this was no normal bear – for ice bears did not talk or give pretty girls golden wreaths. But most had seen the bear with their own eyes taking the princess and knew that bears only did one thing to pretty girls, and that one thing was never a nice thing. They knew that she must be dead. Her parents questioned her, and as always were not at all sure they understood the answers.

Her mother said Astrilde must, on all accounts, find out what the bear looked like when he was a man. Perhaps he *was* really a monster; all would be answered then. Besides, it was improper for her daughter to be sharing a bed with a man she couldn't see. He must be hiding something. But her father said that she must listen to what the bear said and obey. It was a girl's duty to do what she was told, and a man's, or indeed a bear's, duty to know what was right and what was wrong, and if only the women in his household would listen to him and do what they were told, all would be right.

Perhaps he could have been wiser. The queen shut up and agreed, nodding severely at her daughters: a woman's place was a woman's place, she must always do what a man told her to do. The king was pleased. He hadn't seen Batilde swallowing her giggles and was satisfied that all was as it should be. As soon as the queen was alone with Astrilde, she explained that one must always let men *think* they are in charge but that, in life, it was better to ignore them and do what *you* know is right. Men, she explained, were basically overgrown babies that need humouring. It didn't take much to make them happy. Just let them think they are right, agree and carry on. The monster approach having failed, she now took to wondering about what a beautiful man the bear must be. She knew her daughter, and her daughter too could wonder endlessly about his hairy, plump, manly beauty.

A week after he'd left her on Tyr's Day, the great white bear returned. Whilst Astrilde might not quite have skipped down the steps as happily as the first time he called for her, she was very happy to see him and couldn't wait to be back in their bed. As she mounted the bear's back, her mother went to kiss her and slipped a candle into her pocket. 'Just in case my dear,' she whispered.

The journey home was quicker than the first time, for they only felt the need to stop once or twice (possibly even thrice) to make love in the snow. All went well for a while, but then one dark night when the bear became a man, she remembered the candle. She thought of how she longed to gaze on her beloved's face, of how he must be so beautiful, more beautiful indeed than the golden wreath itself; she simply must look upon him. When he was asleep, she tiptoed off and lit her candle. He *was* beautiful, more beautiful than she could ever have imagined, and younger than she had thought – in fact, she doubted that he was much older than her, for the prime of his life was yet to come. She was then overcome with a great longing to see all of him. She gently pulled back the furs to examine every single inch and what she saw pleased her very much. But it also distracted her, and as she studied the most beautiful part of him, in her great joy and awe her hand wobbled. A great stream of molten wax fell from the candle, burning him where no man ever wants to be burnt.

He awoke, furious. He screamed, he yelled, 'You foolish girl, you stupid girl! You have ruined everything! We were weeks away from breaking free of the enchantment, and now I must go and marry the troll hag and never see you and never be happy again!'

It is possible he would not have been quite so furious if he had not been burnt in such a delicate place, but between the pain and the prophesy, fury flowed unabated. There was something about his pure animal anger that was so magnificent, so glorious, that it made her long for him afresh with every bit of her glowing body, but it was not to be. He shook himself. Fur started to grow. His beautiful soft body hardened and encrusted itself with enormous, disgusting muscles. His face elongated, his teeth grew, his hands and fingers stretched, becoming claws and paws; he was a bear again. She pleaded and pleaded, but all he would say was, 'I must go now to the troll hag Aeglief and marry her.' As he left the chamber, she leapt on his back and clung on as he rushed out of the castle and through the snow and ice and the great forest, heading north.

The point came where she could cling no longer and fell in a faint, naked, into the snow. It cannot have been mere chance alone that deposited her there outside a small snug cottage, or chance that alerted the cottagers, who swiftly gathered her up and wrapped her in furs by their fire. As soon as Astrilde came to, she asked anxiously about the white bear. 'Ah yes, he passed, rushing north as he always does, so fast no one can ever catch him. Perhaps you are his love?'

She cried and explained that she must follow him. Then, a little girl spoke up: 'The princess cannot follow him in the snow naked. Let me make her some clothes.' Taking some golden scissors she cut into the air, and with each new cut clothing appeared: first, the finest silk underwear, and then, the warmest seal-skin suit and boots. They made her rest and eat and spend the night. In the morning, the little girl asked if she could give the princess her golden scissors, as they had more clothes than they would ever need. Surely the princess would need them on her quest. With this parting gift, they sent her on her way.

When she had walked north as far as anyone can walk and when she was as close to collapse as anyone can be without actually collapsing – it might have been a day, it might have been a week – she stumbled into a lonely dwelling. A warm fire and anxious cottagers greeted her. 'Oh yes, we've seen the great bear, running north as he always runs north – perhaps you are his love? But you must stop and eat with us and sleep here until you are refreshed. Drink from our little boy's magic bottomless flask, a source of mead sweeter and stronger than anyone has drunk before.'

When she was restored and ready to leave, the little boy spoke up and asked if he could give the princess his flask. They had enough to drink to last their lifetime, and surely she would need it in her quest? With this parting gift, Astrilde set off and walked far, farther than far, until she could walk no longer, collapsing yet again at the door of another conveniently-placed tiny cottage. The cottagers took her in, warmed her up and fed her delicious morsels that appeared on a beautiful little girl's magic tablecloth whenever it was set. They had seen the white bear: 'Oh yes, running north like he always runs north, fast and true, but as one runs to one's own funeral.' When she was strong enough to go on, the little girl piped up and asked if she could give the beautiful princess her magic tablecloth?

With her three magical gifts, Astrilde set off. She was now self-sufficient: with her scissors, she could cut the warmest furs out of the air to sleep in; she could drink of the finest mead from her flask; she could feast of dainties that surpassed any she had eaten in her father's hall. I do not know how long she travelled, for none that I know have travelled that far, but on she went to find her beloved. Eventually she came to a great cliff that stretched up into the sky, to the west and to the east as far as she could see. She couldn't go over it, she couldn't go under it. She would have to try and go around it, but 'round she went, and walked further than she felt anyone had walked before – and still, the cliff loomed in every direction. Then, at the bottom of the cliff, she saw what looked like a little door and knocked and knocked again.

A miserable crone opened the door. 'I suppose you'd better come in,' she said, offering a single grain of salt and a single crumb of bread. The cave was sparse, unfurnished, but kept warm and light with a great fire in the middle. It was full of naked children who, despite the warmth, were all crying, so the lady of the cave could not hear the princess's questions about the bear.

'They are crying because they are hungry, the poor lambs,' she explained.

'Well feed them, then!' demanded Astrilde in the way she spoke to the serfs in her father's hall.

'I suppose I could,' said the crone. She put a great pan on the fire, adding some sticks, moss and pebbles before describing to the children an entirely imaginary and delicious reindeer stew that would be ready soon.

'But that is nonsense, they can't eat that.'

'No, that be true, they can't, but it'll keep them quiet for a bit until it's done and then they will start crying again.'

'If you have no food for them, may I feed them?'

'You are a thin lady with no luggage. With what can you possibly hope to feed so many?'

'With this,' said Astrilde, whipping out her magic tablecloth. The children and the crone ate as if there were no tomorrow. But when Astrilde wanted to ask about the bear, the children were making such a noise that the crone really could not hear.

'Oh, can't you send the children out into the snow to play?' Astrilde demanded imperiously.

'I do not know who or *what* you are,' replied the crone. 'You have fed the children and you have fed me and for that I am very grateful, but I will not send them out naked to freeze to death.' So Astrilde got out her magical scissors and made them all warm clothes, and they rushed joyfully out to play.

'Ah, it is the ice bear, is it? No doubt you are, or were to be, his bride. Well, it is of no use. He has gone up over the cliff into the troll hag Aeglief's kingdom. No mortal can climb up there, or should climb up there, if it comes to that,' said the crone.

After, well, it might have been one glass of mead and it might have been many glasses of mead, the crone relented and said that there *might* be a way. The children's father (who was no friend of hers but liked the children, even going so far as to feed them sometimes) was a smith. If the princess were to make some more warm clothes for them, look after and feed the children, then the crone would go and ask him to make claws like the ice bear's for her hands and feet. Then Astrilde might – she did not think she *could*, but she *might* – be able to climb up that cliff.

Astrilde waited in the cave for many, many days. She occupied her time with making clothes for the children for the rest of their lives, preserving food from the tablecloth and filling jars with mead. Just when she decided that she'd been abandoned with the children and was cursing the crone, the crone reappeared, looking flushed and cheery with freshly-wrought iron claws. Astrilde strapped them to her hands and feet and started to climb. The crone said she'd never make it (and, truth to tell, Astrilde thought she would never make it). But make it she did, in triumph. On top of the cliff, in the far frozen north, she entered another world, a warm world, of great luscious meadows with huge herds of cows, prosperous farms and miserable people who barely answered her, but pointed in the distance to a great, hideous castle.

The troll hag Aeglief was due to be married, she learnt, but she wanted it to be the wedding to end all weddings. Aeglief wanted the most magnificent dress that anyone had ever worn, and her companions had to be gloriously attired, but she was so dissatisfied with the first lot of tailors that she had eaten them all. At that, the other tailors either ran away or were so frightened that their fingers trembled when they tried to sew. Aeglief realised that if she ate them as well, then she would have nothing to wear at all, but was very dissatisfied with the results – which was why the wedding was yet to take place. The same story went for the food and the mead. Aeglief herself would be happy, as she always was, with boiled babies to eat and virgin's blood to drink, but she wanted a feast her subjects and groom could partake in too.

Astrilde quietly sat down in the main square under the looming, hideous, endless castle. With her magic gold scissors she made the most beautiful clothes for all comers. It wasn't long before Aeglief summoned her into her vast hall. To begin with, Astrilde was surprised, overwhelmed even, by its dazzling white walls. She assumed that it was lined with shining white marble, but a closer look revealed that the marble was human bones and skulls delicately arranged in beautiful patterns. But no, she would not sell her scissors to the troll hag. She would *give* them to her, if she could be allowed to spend just one night with her beloved bear. Aeglief pondered. She could eat the little hazelnut, she supposed (and very tasty too, no doubt), but they were magical scissors, and if they were not given freely, they might not work. With those scissors she would have the dress to end all dresses and the court would be dressed finer than any court in history. She had no choice but to agree, though she reserved the right to lull her love, her lovely cuddly bear, to sleep with one of her lullabies.

That night, Astrilde yelled and slapped and did everything that she could to wake the slumbering bear, but the troll hag's special lullaby had been to give him to drink of mandragora, a potent sleeping potion. Nothing would wake him. So the next day, Astrilde set out her magic tablecloth in the square and sold delicious delicacies. Soon

enough, she was summoned to Aeglief, who obtained the tablecloth on the same terms: another night with the beloved bear. Again he was drugged, but this time, a servant happened to hear the wailing and told the bear what had happened – for, I think it is fair to say, few loved Aeglief and most loved and indeed pitied the poor bear. So when Astrilde opened her mead stall on the market and was once again summoned and once again made the bargain with Aeglief, her dear bear was prepared. He only pretended to drink his bedtime cup. A suspicious Aeglief checked that her beloved snoring bear was really unconscious, stabbing him brutally through the arm with a needle, but despite the pain he pretended to snore on, louder and louder.

No sooner was Astrilde in his room than he was awake and she was in his arms. Then, with the servants' help, they sneaked out. They knew they had but little time, for the wedding was to be celebrated the next day. Like all troll weddings, it would take place on the other side of the bottomless chasm on Troll Mountain's sacred summit. He was a clever bear, and he had a plan. He woke the carpenters, who had made the ceremonial bridge for the occasion. The carpenters, and indeed their babies, had not been treated any better by the troll hag Aeglief than the tailors or the cooks, and were more than happy to help.

In the morning, the solemn wedding procession set off. None had ever seen such a beautiful dress (but a troll hag in a beautiful dress, as the saying goes, is still a troll hag). When Aeglief, with her troll bridegrooms and troll guard, were crossing the bridge, a little lever was pulled and the middle opened out, taking her and all her trolls down, down into the bottomless chasm. For all I know, they are falling still. As they fell the enchantment weakened. With every mile they fell, the bear lost fur and bear-ness until he was all man, a glorious man, a real man, a prince amongst men, with his beautiful belly and great big beard. He swept up his princess in his arms, kissed her, took her back to the castle and celebrated their marriage. He then fetched the three children who had helped her; it turned out that they were her lost children. They served as pages and pagesses at the coronation, where Astrilde and the bear were crowned king and queen of the north. They may still be there now, ruling happily ever after, for it is a land outside of time and place, a land where dreams are listened to.

Two little boys dream of gold.
Three enormous trolls dream of boy stew.
Whose lucky day will it be?

Three Trolls, One Eye

ong, long ago, so long ago that no one can quite remember if it really happened or not, on a beautiful fjord in Norway, there was a small town. Just outside this town lived the Andersons, a very, very poor family. Like so many poor families in those days they had lots and lots of children, who they struggled to feed and look after. The children were almost feral, begging, stealing and being a nuisance.

There is, and always has been, a great prejudice against the poor and I'm not sure that this is fair. Why was father Lars Anderson so poor? It was not because he did not work hard every day of his life; it was simply that his master did not pay him well. Whilst the master and his family lived in a big house and dined on meat and fish every day, old Lars and his family lived in a shack and barely ate fish or meat once or twice a year. Ah, I hear you say, Lars must have been very stupid and the master very clever! I wish that were true. I do not indeed know much about the master's intellect - he was so lazy and had done so little since the day he was born that it is hard to say how clever he was - but I would lay odds of ten to one that he was a deeply stupid man. Old Lars I know for a fact was clever and bright, read his Bible every day, could fix and make anything at all. So why was the clever, hardworking man poor and the lazy, stupid man rich? I wish I knew, but I am a storyteller, and this is a book of stories. All I can tell you is that it was ever so and will be so evermore. But I will never be able to tell you the story if I ponder on life's inequalities. I must return to Lars and Ulricka's many, many neglected children.

Once upon a time, long, long ago in Norway, Lars and Ulricka had, among their many children, two boys: Karl, who was twelve, and Ove, who was ten, almost urchins. The brothers were the best of friends and allies in their difficult battle to survive. Their parents had no time, little space and hardly any food for them. This was the time before schools had been invented to steal away childhood and provide employment for sadists and paedophiles, so their days were spent gathering what food they could, playing games and keeping out of their parents' way.

The little town was a fruitful hunting ground. From time to time, people would give them errands, or even buns. Market day was always a good day. Someone would want their shopping carried home, their stall watched, their horses held, cart loaded or unloaded. On a good day, they could even take food back to their family. Despite being boys and poor, they were good, beloved by everyone – not that anyone had much time for them, or wanted to talk to them. They were poor, after all, and dressed in rags and begged. (There has ever been this prejudice against poverty, but the poor can be useful.) There was one lady, who wasn't very nice and smelt and was very old but didn't mind their poverty, who talked to them from behind her mushroom stall. She talked to anyone who would listen – and it was only the boys who did – of all the gold in the mountains above. She told them that there was gold just lying around for the taking, explaining what gold was and what they could do with it.

They asked their father, who said it was an old wives' tale and that, if they ever went near the mountains, he'd beat them black and blue. As he beat them enough when he was drunk, which he often was, and they did not want any more beatings, they did not ask him again. Their older brothers and everyone else they ever asked all agreed, this golden story was nonsense. All told them to stay away from the mountains. The old woman told them the master got *his* gold from the hills, that was why he was rich. That made sense. They could see no other way for a man who rarely lifted a finger to get rich (though I suppose if they'd thought any further, they'd have wondered how he could have got his portly frame up into the mountains in the first place).

As a game, they started talking and dreaming about what they would do with the gold, how they would feed their family, clothe their family, live in a brick house and have fires every day! Blankets even – maybe a pony, lots of ponies, a servant girl or two to help their poor mama.

That summer the dreams got bigger, taking over their lives. Everyone else saw great forbidding and forbidden mountains looming ominously over the small town, but the boys saw gold. By autumn, they couldn't sleep, so they had to go. They snuck what supplies they could – which wasn't much, a hatchet and a tinder box –and went up, up and up. They were used to living off the land. They could find food, make a fire every night, with long, long sticks in it that could be quickly picked up, still flaming, to chase any wild beasts away. But the mountains always seemed so far away. They wondered, as all who walk in mountains do, if they were bewitched? For, every time they got to the top, a new top appeared, and they still seemed as far away as they were when they set off. They kept cheerful by telling themselves stories about how happy everyone would be when they got home with all the gold.

Finally they were in the mountains. In their dreams, in the old woman's tales, the gold had just been lying around for the picking, and they'd brought bags to fill. Now, I know there was gold in those mountains, but it wasn't just growing on the trees for picking like so many autumn apples, so they couldn't see it. They started to talk instead of how much trouble they'd be in, the beatings they'd get when they got home. They couldn't go home without gold, but soon they realised they couldn't stay long in the mountains. Winter was coming. It was getting cold, food was scarce, they missed their mother; they'd have to go back.

That night, strange noises and the tremblings of the earth woke them from their slumbers by the fire. They looked at each other and Karl grabbed the hatchet. The ground moved and the sounds got louder. It was unlike any wild beasts they'd ever heard, deep and guttural – like a pig perhaps, but a pig whose grunts shook the forest. They both knew what it must be and trembled. Then, above the wind, they heard the terrible words, the words all children dread, the words that children may well hear if they are not asleep by eight o'clock, or the end of this story, whichever comes first:

'FEE-FI-FO-FUM, I SMELL THE BLOOD OF A CHRISTIAN!'

It was forest trolls, hungry forest trolls, hunting for children; trolls with the scent of their dinner in their nostrils. Fire would not protect from trolls. Karl grabbed the hatchet and told Ove to run, run like the wind to get out of there.

'You may make it!' he said.

'I will do my best!'

'Don't look back, *run!*'

Ove did not need to be told twice.

'Oooh I can see my dinner!'

'I can smell my dinner!'

'Yummy yum yum – fried or roasted boy tonight?'

Karl could hear three voices. Then, he could see three enormous trolls stumbling through the forest, each holding onto the other. They stopped and argued for a bit. The leader took one enormous eye from the socket in the centre of his forehead and passed it to the next, who put it in his socket and took the lead. There were three trolls with but one eye between them. They were stumbling after Ove and, slow as they were, a slow troll is faster than a boy.

Karl crept through the forest. He snuck up behind and, with his hatchet, neatly severed the Achilles tendon of first one troll and then another who, lame and in pain, clung desperately to the third so that they all fell in a heap with the eye tumbling down. Karl grabbed the eye and stood back to watch the fun. After a while, the trolls' hands started feeling desperately around them. Karl called out, bold as brass: 'Do you want your eye back?'

'Who is that?'

'It's dinner!'

'It's a boy – it's a walking casserole.'

'It's meatballs on legs.'

'Roast boy!'

'Boy sausages.'

'Boy steaks!'

They were all salivating, great lakes of spit coming out of their disgusting toothless mouths.

'It's our dinner, and it's talking...'

'And it's got our eye!'

'Oy, dinner, give us back our eye!'

'No!' he replied. Sneaking forward, he cut off the little toe of the closest troll and set fire to the trousers of the next, just for a laugh. When they had calmed down, he demanded gold in return for the eye. They weren't the easiest creatures to talk to, but eventually they told him the gold was in their cave and if he'd lead them back, they'd give it to him. He said he didn't know the way. 'Well,' they said, 'give us back the eye.'

As I have said, Karl may have been poor, but he was not stupid. He saw the trail the enormous creatures had made through the forest and, following their footsteps in reverse, he led them to the cave. There, they found the old woman from the market rubbing her hands with glee and preparing an enormous pot. She said it was all ridiculous: he was a boy, a piece of meat, their dinner, and she wasn't going to give him any gold, she was going to cook him and eat him. But Karl said if she came any closer, he'd cut the eye in two and throw it off the cliff. So she gave him gold and he told the trolls the eye was on the ground in front of them. The first rushed for it and fell off the edge of the cliff. Unfortunately, the other two were holding onto him and they too fell to their deaths.

All that is left to say is that Karl and Ove returned home, and they and their family lived happily ever after. Not that I want you to go away with the impression that gold buys happiness, but in this case it did.

She had twelve daughters but longed for a son. Magic onions bring her two boys, but the eldest must first survive the wilderness and kill many girls before an evil lady tries to sacrifice her unwanted stepdaughter to him, and he finds love and his rightful throne. To be continued.

The Serpent Prince

nce upon a time, long, long ago, there a was a glorious king and a glorious queen. They were happy as only good people can be. They loved each other and they loved their people, who loved them in return. They ruled wisely, and where the ruler is wise and happy, his people follow. All was for the best in this best-of-all-possible worlds.

...Except of course it wasn't, for if it had been, that would be the end of my story. I could have just written, 'Once upon a time they all lived happily ever after,' but they didn't, or not yet anyway, so I *do* get to tell you a story after all. For there was an absence at the heart of the country, an absence in the royal castle, a worm in the middle of an otherwise beautiful cheese: the king and queen had no son. Daughters are all very well, and they had twelve of those, but a son was needed – for who would take over the kingdom when they were gone?

The king and queen tried to count their blessings and listen to those who told them what a nuisance sons were. Their neighbourly king, Nikompompus, the queen's brother, would come and try to cheer them up by telling them, at length, about his twelve naughty boys and how he longed for a daughter. Just *one* daughter. They came to hate these visits.

An old crone started coming to the castle and asking to see the queen, but as she did not say why, and as she smelt, they refused her. She came again and again and again, until one day, the queen was passing by and wanted to know what the fuss was about. 'Ahh,' cried out the old crone, 'if you'll only listen to me, my dear, you shall have your heart's desire.'

Luckily for the crone, the queen was feeling rather bored and invited her in. The crone told her that she would give birth to two boys. The queen laughed and said she was far too old. 'Not at all, not at all,' replied the crone. 'When you have your bath tonight, two onions will be there. Peel and eat them.'

The queen, whilst wondering how the crone knew it was that night of the year, dismissed her with rather a small coin and a smile before forgetting all about it. That evening as she luxuriated in her marble bath, two onions popped out of the tap. As you would (or certainly *I* would), she grabbed the first and ate it straight away. Then, remembering that the crone had told her to peel them, she peeled the next one and gobbled it up.

Anyone who has ever eaten two raw onions in quick succession will know what comes next. Her loins burnt with an insatiable desire. She tried the soap, but it was not what she needed. She needed a man. She leapt out of the bath, put her robe over her still-dripping body and rushed downstairs, where she found the king drinking with his friends. He knew what that look in her eyes meant, even if he had not seen it for many a year. She grabbed his hand and dragged him to her chamber, where she pushed him violently onto her bed. She pulled off his trousers, went down on her knees quickly to get him ready, then vigorously rode him like she'd ride a wild horse, all night long. (Well, let us not overdo it. They had both passed their fortieth birthdays, after all.) They had not had so much fun since the last time she had been drunk five years ago. One thing led to another, and they rediscovered the joy of their youth. No one saw them for a week – but all saw the queen's belly when it began to grow, and grow it did. It was *enormous*.

When her confinement came around nine months later, as was usual in those days, it was just the queen and a midwife. The queen strained and yelled. The midwife bent to help. She looked, she looked again. Out of the queen's punani slithered a snake. Quick as a flash, she grabbed it and threw it out the window into the moat. 'What was that?' asked the queen. 'Only weewee,' replied the midwife. Before the queen could stop and think she had to yell, and then a boy came tumbling out. A beautiful boy, the apple of everyone's eye.

He was beautiful as only a boy can be beautiful, loved as only a boy can be. I would like to say that he was good and kind like his parents, but he wasn't. I don't mean to say he was bad or nasty or mean, just a little stupid, that was all. (It's nobody's fault, being stupid. For the stupid person, it is a bit like being dead. You haven't a clue what is going on, but it is a tragedy for those all around you. There's not a lot you can do with a stupid boy. Besides, the worst kings, rulers, politicians et cetera are often very intelligent. A stupid man can still be a good king.)

The king and queen thought the best thing they could do was find an intelligent wife for him once he was old enough, that is to say sixteen. Unfortunately, the day before their wedding, the girl they found was bitten by a snake and died. Three years later they tried again. This time, the bride-to-be fell in a well and drowned. Nobody knew why, but I know why: she saw a snake, screamed, stepped backwards and fell down the well.

Somehow or other, every intended bride died. Eventually, when the prince was approaching the prime of his life, that is to say his mid- to late-fifties, the king and queen sent him to see the local wise woman. Like every medical practitioner from the dawn of time to the present day, she first made him pee in a jug. She smelt it, looked in it, tasted it and shook her head. It was all cloudy, very cloudy, she said. She couldn't see why, but there was something stopping him marrying in the kingdom. He must look elsewhere for his bride.

He set off for the nearest kingdom but one (the nearest king, if you remember, only had sons). In the great forest near the border, the coach stopped. A nervous coachman reported a great snake in the way. The prince was furious. 'Drive on!' he commanded, hitting the coachman. But the coach did not move. The prince leapt out and, with horror, saw an enormous serpent rearing over him.

'Erm, get out of the way, erm, please,' he stuttered.

'Where are you going?' hissed the serpent.

'None of your business, now bugger off.'

'I know where you are going and why, but you will never be married until I am married,' the serpent hissed. 'Now go home.'

The prince turned tail and fled. He made a few other attempts to leave the kingdom, but the serpent would not let him pass. So, as the court always did when in doubt, they consulted the wise woman, who told them to find a bride for the serpent. Thinking the serpent wouldn't be very fussy, they asked Mad Mary, who said no. Then, they reminded her that she was due to be hung for drowning her baby and promised she wouldn't be hung if she married the serpent, so she said yes.

The serpent was summoned, married to Mad Mary and led to a dirty room above a stable. The next morning, her bloody corpse was found. A few more brides were rounded up and all suffered the same fate. No more women could be persuaded to enter into holy matrimony with a serpent, so billboards were plastered all over the kingdom:

LARGE SERPENT SEEKS WIFE.
THE KING AND QUEEN WILL PROVIDE AN EXCELLENT DOWRY. APPLY AT THE ROYAL CASTLE.

There were a couple of enquiries but none serious, until the news reached Mrs Knauss. Or rather, the second Mrs Knauss – the first having died and been replaced by her maid, a nasty woman who had promised to love and look after the young mistress Alvide, who was beautiful and good. But once the second Mrs Knauss had given birth to her own daughter, Bergdis, who was as ugly and evil as Alvide was good, Mr Knauss died, and then they were both horrible to poor Alvide.

Mrs Knauss immediately set out for the castle and begged an audience. She hoped, she prayed she was not too late. Her daughter, the beautiful, the good Alvide, had seen the notice and begged her on bended knees to go and enquire. Alvide had always loved snakes, she lied, never had Alvide been interested in anything else. This was her dream come true! Oh, how she hoped that she wasn't too late, that it was still possible for her daughter to be considered.

Oh it was true, too true, that Alvide was not a noble lady. But, she said, showing them a picture, she was very beautiful and so in love with snakes. Why, if she was the chosen one, it would make her heart explode with happiness.

The king and queen were desperate and delighted. Mrs Knauss asked if they might humour her greatly-loved daughter and send a carriage with a large guard of soldiers to escort her back in style, for Alvide so longed to ride in a carriage and loved nothing more (except for serpents, of course) than a man in uniform. The king and queen, not wishing this dream to escape them, readily agreed. Mrs Knauss returned home, marched into the house and told Alvide that she was to be married to the serpent and to be jolly grateful too. She had no choice. The king had sent the army to bring her back, just look out the window. Well, she *did* have a choice; she could be killed by one of the soldiers. Seeing no escape, poor Alvide threw herself on her mother's grave in the garden and cried herself to sleep. The tears seeped through the soil to her mother's bones, forming a new umbilical cord down which the soul of her dead (but by no means departed) mother told her what to do.

The next morning, Alvide was ever so cheerful. She instructed the captain of the guards to get the jewels that her dear kind step-mama had kept safe for her all these years, and those seven beautiful silk dresses in the wardrobe. Mrs Knauss tried to protest, but she could not deny that the jewels had belonged to her predecessor and were Alvide's by right. Alvide had no claim to the dresses, but the captain was stern, and Mrs Knauss comforted herself by thinking that she'd soon have them back, once the serpent had eaten her troublesome stepdaughter. When Mrs Knauss mounted the carriage, Alvide shrieked in horror and commanded the captain throw her out, for she was nothing but her father's scullery maid, and an ugly old woman to boot.

By the time they arrived at the royal castle Alvide had transformed herself into a mighty lady, and by her very airs commanded respect. She demanded to be shown the marriage bed, sniffed and said that she needed a room in the castle, not some cockroach-infested lair above a stable. The first room she was shown was not nearly good enough. She haughtily demanded bigger and better until, at last, she was given a great chamber, with an enormous bed. This, she said, would do, but she did not like the round posts on the bed, she didn't like round things. If she wanted to sleep in a wood, she'd sleep in a wood. The posts needed to be squared off with nice sharp corners. The fire would need to be lit. She would need several large blocks of soap, those big scrubbing brushes from the stable, that great marble bath filled with hot water. If they wouldn't do all of that, she would not marry the serpent.

There was something about her imperious ways that made them follow her orders. Besides, the servants smirked amongst themselves, she'd be dead soon enough. She demanded a proper wedding ceremony with a proper wedding feast, all of which took a couple of weeks to prepare. On the wedding day, she looked ridiculous: she'd dressed in all seven of her stepmother's silk gowns. Still the king took her arm and led her to the altar, where the serpent awaited and the holy vows of matrimony were sworn. After the feasting, her serpent groom led her to the bridal chamber and locked the door. He looked at her, his great forked tongue slithering in and out of his repulsive mouth. He would have leered if a serpent could leer. He was going to have fun with her first. She looked like a piece of alright, not like the others. Oh yes, he'd have some fun with her first.

'Sssssssssssstrip,' he hisssssssssssssed, 'take your clothes off.'

'You first,' she replied, commandingly.

This took him aback. No one had ever asked him to get naked before. He looked at her, and as she looked particularly delicious and imperious, he shrugged what passed for his shoulders. He slithered up to the bed and started rubbing vigorously against the sharpened corners until his skin began to peel and a complete layer of shed skin lay at the foot of the bed.

'Your turn,' he hissed.

She took one dress off and looked at him. He rubbed another layer of skin off, and so it went until he took the seventh layer off and collapsed into a bloody, shapeless mess on the floor. Not wanting to get her last dress dirty, Alvide took it off. Naked now, she scooped up the bloody mess in her arms, got into the bath and scrubbed and soaped and scrubbed and soaped and scrubbed and soaped until out of the mess popped a devastatingly handsome prince. He was a

man in the prime of his life, that is to say, his late fifties, a real man, a proper man with a great beard and long hair, a prince's body, a proper body, not one of those labouring men's bodies, all muscle and hard sinew, nothing to get hold of. Oh no – a real man's body, with delightful lumps and squishy bits to hold onto and lay a head, not one of those strong men you can't dominate. He was every young woman's dream of the perfect man. It was their marriage night, but I am not going to pander to your prurient curiosity by going into all the sordid details of that legendary night of passion. Instead, I will leave a discreet gap below for you to fill with your filthy thoughts.

Dear, gentle reader, you are invited to fill the space below with your obscene thoughts describing their marriage night. Or draw a picture. I wanted an illustration, but the publisher rejected my brief as they said it would be too obscene for your gentle eyes (though I think it was really because they don't want it to be a top-shelf publication) – but this is your book; you can put what you like in it. Should your mind be blank, or your curiosity not of a prurient nature, you may skip this stage:

Suffice it for me to say that the next day, as was customary, the bloodied sheet was flown from the flagstaff at the top of the tallest tower so all would know that she'd been a virgin on her wedding night.

The next morning, the servants were surprised to see a great bloody mess of snakeskin on the floor and reported that Alvide had eaten the serpent. The king and queen rushed in to be greeted by the handsome prince, who said, 'Hello, Mummy and Daddy, do you recognise me now?'

He told them the story of his birth and wild years as a serpent in the forest. They called the wise woman, who called the midwife, who corroborated the story and was promptly hung by order of the new crown prince. The old crown prince was told that it was now safe for him to go and look for a bride elsewhere, but nothing more was heard from him. It is possible, indeed probable, that he met with some accident and died somewhere in the forest not very far from the castle. The king and queen, who, to be fair, were rather elderly by now so it might have been natural, soon died, and the serpent prince was crowned king. As king he was, if we want to be kind to him (and I rather think we do), overcome with remorse for the way he'd won his kingdom and all the people he'd killed, on his priest's orders, he set out on a pilgrimage for the Holy Land, leaving a heavily-pregnant Alvide behind.

If you remember, the serpent prince had twelve sisters. Ten of them were by now happily married and had gone abroad to breed more princes and princesses. But in every clutch there is normally a dud, and in a clutch of fourteen, it is no surprise that there were three duds. The stupid brother has already disappeared from the story and ten of the sisters married, but two remain: the twins Aslaug and Signe, and to listen to them, let alone look at them, this would come as no surprise. Unfortunately they were not stupid, but they were ugly, evil and plain nasty. (Now if I was being kind, I would say that they were not born bad, that nature made them ugly and nurture turned them bad. They'd been teased, prodded and poked since birth. Their ten sisters, having all found love and happiness, had crowed over their misfortune. Had they not been princesses, who are supposed to be beautiful, had they not had ten beautiful sisters, had they had no sisters at all, had they had parents who'd loved them, brothers who'd cherished them, then I have no doubt at all that they would have been good.)

The two ugly sisters, with their beautiful sisters all married and departed, an unmarried, stupid crown prince and elderly parents, had slowly taken control of the court. They made a great public show of fealty and devotion to the new king and queen, but inwardly they hated them. With the king away, they could plot the queen's ruin. Alvide was no fool, but she had not grown up at court and had no allies, apart from the captain who'd first brought her there and was her devoted servant. When the time came for her confinement, they insisted that they and they alone would tend to their dear, much beloved sister. Alvide gave birth to a beautiful boy, but the sisters announced that she had given birth to a deformed kitten and must be a witch and must be burnt. They kept her under lock and key in a tower, unable to burn her without the king's orders. On hearing the news the king was saddened, but remembering that he had been born a serpent, sent back orders that she was not to be harmed until his return.

The terrible twins needed her dead. They filled the court with their cronies, producing endless reports of the evil the witch queen was doing. They smuggled a lion cub in from a passing circus, pretending it was her son grown huge. The cronies all wrote terrible accounts to the king, begging that she and the kitten be burnt at once, for, even confined in the deepest dungeon, held by the thickest chains, she was working her magic. The kitten grew and grew and killed all who came near. If it grew any bigger, they would not be able to confine it any longer and it would break out and kill everyone! They called it Fenris Cat. They fed the lion locals and returned the half-eaten bodies, explaining that the queen's son, the kitten, had escaped again. The people of the kingdom petitioned the king to rid them of this witch. Reluctantly, he sent back orders for the burning of his son and wife.

Fortunately, it was the queen's only friend and ally, the kind captain, who came to do the burning. He burnt a pig and piglet instead and sent the queen and prince to live with his old nanny in a secret cottage deep in the woods. When the king returned, the captain led him to his queen and son. The king's anger knew no bounds. The ugly sisters and all who had enabled them were burnt on an enormous pyre. Only then could the serpent king, his bride and son live happily ever after.*

* I have been telling this story for many years. One day, someone rushed up to me and said it wasn't Norwegian at all, it was Swedish. However, the story is so old that I'm not sure if it is possible to talk of Norwegian and Swedish things in the depths of time. But it did worry me, so I didn't tell it again for a few years. When I did, a lady with a beautiful accent came running up to say it was a Hungarian tale. At this point, I put my hands in the air and say I really don't care where it is from: it is a wonderful story and *I* first heard it in Norway. I have never really believed in nations and nationalities when it comes to people anyhow – an artificial construct created after the French Revolution, when rulers could no longer rely on the divine right of kings and created new myths – and if they don't apply to people they shouldn't apply to stories either.

PAPUA NEW GUINEA

A saying from the cassowary to her chicks:
'Whatever falls from above is always
the fruit of the tree, take and eat, but avoid
anything from the ground moving towards you,
because it will bring you harm.'

Proverb heard in Mount Hagen

Bury me in Papua New Guinea. It is my second home, the place I love the most. If I wasn't married with four children and a host of other obligations tying me down, I would go there, stay there, live there and die there. New Guinea is the world's second-largest island, home to the third-largest rainforest as well as a quarter of the world's languages, fauna and flora found nowhere else, glaciers and coral reefs, orchids and ferns, shells and birds, crocodiles and constrictors, butterflies and walking sticks.

Since I was small, I dreamt of New Guinea. I read David Attenborough's book and saw his television programs. I read Tim Flannery, Vojtech Novotny, Jared Diamond, Errol Flynn's memoirs, Margaret Mead, Bronisław Malinowski, Tobias Schneebaum, Peter Matthiessen; I watched the documentary *Dead Birds*. Anything and everything I could find, I devoured. I visited London's Museum of Mankind. I went to the great museums in Paris, Berlin, Amsterdam and of course the Metropolitan in New York, with its mind-blowing Michael C. Rockefeller Wing filled with Asmat masterpieces (never imagining in my wildest dreams that, one day, *today* in fact, I would be sitting writing this, in my library, overlooked by Asmat shields, drums, an Mbis pole, Sepik masks and canoe prows, Malagan carvings from New Ireland, Lake Sentani carvings and magnificent highland bilums, all collected on my many expeditions to New Guinea). I looked for a guidebook. It seemed dangerous and prohibitively expensive for someone of my modest means to travel there alone.

Then, in 2013, I met the great explorer Stewart McPherson, who invited me on an expedition to search for lost carnivorous plants, the Nepenthes I grow and love. I entered a world I had only ever dreamt about. We chartered a small plane, trekked and camped deep in the rainforest, snorkelled on the world's richest coral reefs, woke at 2 a.m., walked up into the hills to wait at dawn for Wilson's bird-of-paradise to clear his display area and dance. I wanted to go again, I *needed* to go, but I had not the funds. So, with Stewart's help, I started my tour company, Gone with the Wynd, in 2018, and I now spend a month of every year there. From the moment I board the Air Niugini flight in Hong Kong or Singapore to the moment I leave, the biggest smile is upon my face. It is the people I meet there that I love the most.

I love to shop, and I love to buy the extraordinary carvings, bags and necklaces they make in Papua New Guinea. With over eight hundred languages, there are two lingua francas there: Tok Pisin, which deceptively looks and sounds familiar (but try to listen and you are lost), and English. Even in the remotest villages, there is nearly always someone who speaks English, someone who worked in a city once. Or, if no one, then someone who speaks Tok Pisin and a guide to translate. I first heard the stories in this chapter in the Sepik and on the Trobriand Islands.

In New Guinea I have witnessed ceremonies, felt the presence of spirits, lived a life I can imagine living nowhere else. I've travelled the length of the island, from the Raja Ampat to the Trobriands, trekked in the highlands both sides of the border, seen more species of birds-of-paradise than I can remember, slept in village houses around the hearth stone, spent weeks in dugout canoes and camped on beaches, forests and mountains. I've flown for hours over virgin rainforest. I've swum in lakes, rivers, waterfalls and more seas than I can remember the names of. I have met so many people whom I would love to call my friends. But I have seen nothing yet; I know nothing yet. I look at the map and I see all the places I have never been and I long, I *long*, to go there. If I had a hundred lifetimes, I could never experience everything I want to experience in New Guinea.

Viktor Wynd
in Aseki, Papua
New Guinea,
November 2019.

Some men are very, very stupid. This is a story about one of these men, why he should have listened to his wife in the beginning and why, as all women should know, a stupid man makes the best husband.

The Man Whose Wife Was Married to the Moon

long, long time ago, a young woman called Mbapata was looking for a husband. She made a long list of what she wanted from a man. She wanted him to be strong, to be kind, to be clever, to be handsome, to be faithful, to protect her, to look after her and to provide for her. In those days it was not often that a woman would choose her own husband, for not only were there not that many people around to choose from, but women were expected to do what they were told. (Bear in mind this story was told to me by a man, and when I asked a 'meri' – the Tok Pisin word for 'woman' – she roared with laughter and said women had always made the decisions, but men were only happy if they thought *they* made them, so were left in blissful ignorance.) Be that as it may, when Mbapata went through the list with her girlfriends, they all fell about laughing and told her if she were to look for just one thing on the list, and then if she was very lucky, she might get lucky.

Mbapata looked at all the eligible men in the village and realised her girlfriends were right, so she settled on Walima. I should say right now that she did not choose him for his brains or his looks. Truth be told (and here I will only tell truth, no lies, or at least I will tell you the stories that I was told, but I can never vouch for the honesty of the person who told it to me – he was, after all, a storyteller), Walima was not hard to get. He was strong, hardworking and could beat any two or three other men in the village – which, if he'd minded being the butt of every joke going, would have meant he was constantly fighting – but he had one attribute Mbapata had not originally wanted, an attribute that all should look for in a potential spouse. He was good-humoured and, liking laughter, cared little that it was so often directed at him. 'A laugh's a laugh for all that,' he would chuckle, when for the twentieth time that night he would rush out in his war paint answering the fake alarm call, or go and have earnest conversations with a tree he was told could talk, or climb up a tree in order to poo to stop the worms crawling up his bum, or try to climb the nettle tree where he was promised there were lots of sago worms but found nothing but nettles, or turn his canoe upside down in order to paddle it quietly, or stick his willy in an ant's nest because his brother said it would feel good, or dig a hole in the midday sun because the sun would burn the hole for him, or gather wet plants from the river to light a fire, or hop all day on one leg to attract a cassowary.

No woman had ever looked at Walima before, so when Mbapata started making eyes at him and sidling up, trying to chat and take his hand, he didn't know what she was about. He might even have suspected a joke, a suspicion not helped when Mbapata wasn't able to stop herself from laughing and had to run away. So she went to his sister who all the world knew looked after him, never teased him and loved him dearly. She was the one he always went to when he couldn't laugh at himself anymore. She would patch up his wounds, warn him when it was a joke and rarely, if ever, laugh at him (well, except for the time when he put his willy in the ant's nest, or ate wallaby poo thinking it was nuts, or got the stick stuck up his arse trying to pull the worms out, or buried himself so that he could grow like a yam, or went arse first into the bush because he'd been told it would attract a pig). Alright, she *did* laugh at him, but only gently, and was always there to comfort him.

She too assumed it was a joke. After all, why would the pretty, popular Mbapata want to marry her dumb brother? 'He's strong,' said Mbapata. 'He'll protect me, he won't beat me, he'll work hard, he'll provide. And I know for a fact that no other girls in the village fancy him, so I don't have to worry about him being unfaithful.'

Walima paid the bride price and that was that. Mbapata didn't worry about him being ugly. The tropical nights were long and very dark and made for loving. As her mother said, all men look the same in the dark, and it's dark half of the time. You can always close your eyes in the day if it comes to that – which, in the first passions of their marriage, it often did. Not that she always closed her eyes, mind; she loved her husband, loved him for his faults, warts and all.

Here is demonstrated a universal truth, for the prejudice against ugly people is unjust. I say this as the reformed founder of the League Against Ugly People, so I know whereof I speak. True, no one wants an ugly friend, no one wants to look at an ugly person, no one wants an ugly child. But this is based on a lie: you no more need to be beautiful on the outside to be beautiful on the inside than you need to be ugly on the outside to be ugly on the inside. In short, looks have nothing to do with it. Don't scorn them. Beauty is a wondrous thing, but beauty tells us nothing: nice to look at, rarely interesting to talk to and with no practical application. Besides, if you truly love someone, even the ugliest ogre becomes beautiful. (I once asked an ugly couple what they said to each other in bed and it turned out that they were just as besotted by their hideous bodies and faces as the next couple, a pair of models, were by theirs. I am not a priest and this is not a sermon, but remember this, if you remember nothing else I tell you: beauty is only skin deep, there's nothing wrong with ugliness. ...On second thought, I'm not sure why *this* should be the only thing you remember, and I doubt that just because I tell you something is true you will believe me and change your wicked ways. I used to want to change the world, but I've given up now, I just want to enjoy it, so I'll get back to Mbapata and Walima.)

Walima built her a good house, cleared a garden and brought meat to the table (a figurative table here, for tables were then unknown). He was definitely not unfaithful and provided that one thing that brings joy to life, laughter, on a daily, even hourly, basis. Sometimes Mbapata wondered if he was just playing stupid to get laughs, but he wasn't. He was really, really stupid. So when, one day, he noticed she was bleeding out of her you-know-what, he roared with anger, demanding to know who she'd been fucking. She laughed and told him not to be silly. She was touched that he was jealous, but he got crosser and the third time he asked, she realised she had to answer. He'd never beaten her before, never even thought about beating her, but he was big, strong and very, very angry, so she had to say something or she didn't know what might happen. She told him she was married to the moon, that all women were married to the moon. The moon came every month. He'd been there last night, and he went to every woman every month.

'But you are not every woman. You are my wife and you will not fuck the moon!' Walima thundered in fury. He swore he would fight Mr Moon when he came again, but that night, unable to sleep for jealous fury, he set off early to track the moon. He knew where the moon was. It was tethered to the great tree where the river met the sea. A few warriors kept him company on the journey, egging him on and laughing, but Walima didn't laugh, he was serious. When, at last, they found the great tree, towering above all others on the seashore, the moon was dangling from a rope above it in the sky. 'Oy moon, you fucked my wife, come down and fight me!' roared Walima.

The moon said nothing. The moon was asleep, dreaming of all the women in the world. But the dream turned nasty. The women were getting bigger and pushing him away. They were swelling, turning into balls. He bounced off them. They grew prickles and spiked him and he really, really needed a wee. He woke up to find Walima yelling at him.

'What do you want, little man?'

'You fucked my wife! Come down and fight me.'

Mr Moon had just been asleep and didn't want to be awake, or troubled by lunatics. 'Go away, little man, go home. I sleep with all the women in the world, always have done, always will do.'

'Come down and fight.'

'She was my wife first. I slept with her first, so you are sleeping with my wife, but I don't mind. NOW GO HOME, LITTLE MAN.'

Walima had been insulted many times in his life and he'd never liked it, but he'd never been called 'little man' before, and he was not a little man. His companions urged him on; they told him not to stand there and be insulted like that. He decided that, if the moon wouldn't come down to him, he'd go up and fight it in the air. He climbed the great tree and then started to climb the rope. The rope went up and up and up and up, but he never seemed to get any closer. Eventually, exhausted, he fell down into the sea. His companions – once they'd stopped laughing – said it was time to go home now. 'Yes, go home now, little man, and give my love to your wife,' bellowed Mr Moon.

After that there was no way Walima was going to give up, though he was weak and needed to find and kill a bushpig to build his strength up for a second attempt. Having had their laughs, his companions went back to the village, where everyone laughed – well almost everyone, Walima's sister didn't laugh...okay, she *did* laugh a bit, but when her brother didn't come home after a week, she set off to look for him. At the great tree, where the river meets the sea, she saw the moon hanging from its rope but did not see Walima. Then she looked again. High, high up the rope she saw a little dot climbing. As she watched, it fell into the sea and an exhausted Walima swam to land. She put both her hands on her hips and told him not to be ridiculous. All women, she said, were married to the moon. 'Even *I* am married to the moon. Live with it! Now *come home*.'

His sister had spoken. He obeyed, and they all lived happily ever after.

Scorned by his one true love, a boy cuts a baby out of her mother's tummy and tries to marry her, but she floats away. Will he find her? Will she marry him – and what will the sun have to say about it all?

The Discovery of the Moon

As there must be over a thousand different peoples on the island of New Guinea, each with their own culture and mythology, so there are a thousand different stories about a thousand different moons. I'm a lunatic and very fond of tales about the moon, so here is another one.

Once upon a time, long, long ago on the Sepik River, a boy called Arowaku was born. This was a time before any white man had been seen or heard of there, and whilst that doesn't have to be so long ago – maybe four or five generations – I have a feeling this took place a *very*, very long time ago. In those days, conflicts between the villages and the different peoples on the river were a part of everyday life, so no one was surprised when Arowaku's father was killed and eaten in a fight with the village next door but one. Naturally, his mother needed a new husband. And, just as naturally, this new husband had less interest in this son than his own progeny, who came thick and fast.

For the most part, children were left to their own devices, except when they could usefully help mind a baby, fillet fish, pound sago or weed a garden. And in those far-off days of plenty, work was by no means as all-consuming as it is for us today. Suffice it to say, Arowaku grew up with even less parental supervision than normal and was able to pursue his one interest singleheartedly. He was one of those children who fixate on one thing and one thing only, be it cars, trains, the periodic table, stamps, coins, butterflies, bugs, reptiles, fish, dinosaurs, cacti, orchids, ferns, skulls, birds, pets, chickens, ducks, seaweed, moss, fungi, books, drawing, seashells, writing...well those are some, but not all, of the obsessions I had as a child. Not that I am pretending to have grown up or out of any of them! But where I had, indeed have, a lot of hobbies, he had but one: he wished to be the greatest hunter in the village. He ignored all requests for help and communal duty by disappearing into the forest to hunt.

The elders might tut and shake their heads, but Arowaku knew that as long as he regularly returned with a cassowary, bushpig, cuscus or bird to share, then he would always be welcome at someone's house whenever it was time to eat. Meat was scarce and even if people did not like him, disapproved of him, criticised his lazy ways, they wanted his meat, and so tolerated him. All was fine for a while, until he reached the age when he desired a wife. As the greatest hunter in the village, he felt he could pick who he liked, and he liked Kwariag. She might well have been happy enough to walk with him in the village, or she might have felt no harm would come of it, or she might have liked to eat the choice birds he brought her, but when he suggested marriage, she roared with laughter. 'Me, marry you? The laziest man in the village, a man who carries his bed on his back with him?' she said, affectionately brushing off some of the sand that still stuck to his back. 'No, thank you very much. I need a man who can garden, build a house and look after me, not a good-for-nothing, lie-about bum!' Cackling, she left him fuming with anger.

Arowaku decided that he would show her. He could do all the other things that other men did and do them better. He'd start with gardening. He didn't know anything about it but knew it involved digging, so he marched off to the gardens and began to dig a hole. He dug and he dug. The whole village turned out to see the man who had never worked digging and the whole village laughed, which only made him dig and dig. The novelty soon wore off and he was left alone to dig. Kwariag, feeling guilty, brought him food, which he disdained, asking only for betel nut and water. He drank greedily before getting on with his digging. She left him to it, and he dug through the night. When dawn came with her rosy fingers, he saw something gleaming in the mud. Realising it was an enormous kina shell (a large, shiny slice taken from a gold-lipped oyster shell and used in New Guinea as currency), he seized it with a great cry of joy.

He held up the great slice of shell. In a blind fugue he marched back to the village, taking the shell to wash in the river. The villagers followed him, calling out to know what it was. 'It is the *biggest and the greatest* kina shell in the world!' he cried. 'Only I, Arowaku, the greatest hunter and the greatest digger, have such a kina, and I will now marry who I choose.'

But the nearer he got to the river, the bigger the 'shell' grew. As he went down into the waters to bathe, it swelled. Then, it just floated out of his hands. Looking up into it, he saw the beautiful silvery face of a woman. From the shore, one of the elders cried out that they could see a spirit in the shell. 'I am Arowaku, the greatest hunter and the greatest digger. I am too great to marry one of you! I am going to marry a spirit,' he announced. 'Marry me!' he called up to the floating sphere.

'Who, who are you?' replied the silvery woman.

'I am Arowaku, the greatest hunter and the greatest digger. I dug you up and I am going to marry you.'

'Marry you? You cruel, cruel man. Marry the man who cut me out of my mother – the earth's – belly? Never. My name is moon and I am destined to marry the sun. But you cut me out early and now my back will never shine. *The spirits will punish you.*'

So saying, the spirit he had taken for a kina shell floated off, up and away. Arowaku gathered his dogs and his spears and set off in pursuit. She soon disappeared, but he did not give up – he never gave up on a chase, he always got his prey, he was the greatest hunter the village had ever known. But the moon left no trace. He hunted here, he hunted there, he hunted up, he hunted down, he hunted by day, he hunted by night. Days, weeks, months went by, and he got thinner and weaker. Finally he remembered the forbidden valley, where man may not go and spirits alone dwell. That would be the place, he thought.

The valley was a kind of paradise, up above what we now call Blackwater Lakes. No person had ever entered, and the animals had no fear of man; he could take as many as he could eat. He slowly recovered his strength and continued his search. In the evening, he

came to a waterfall at the far end of the valley. In that waterfall he saw a woman standing with her back to him, the water crashing onto it. He called out but she could not hear, so he sat and watched. Feasting his eyes on her naked body, his loins stirred and a hunger within him grew and grew. Finally, she stepped out of the waterfall and turned towards him. He gasped. Her front was not black like his skin was black; it was a glowing silver.

'Marry me!' he called.

'Who are you?'

'I am Arowaku, the greatest hunter and the greatest digger. I dug you out of the earth.'

'I cannot marry you. I must marry the sun when my back is clear and shines like my front.'

'Marry *me*.'

'Why would I marry you? I am a spirit, I live forever. You, you are gone in a blinking of an eye. Leave this place, the spirits will punish you.'

'Marry me!'

'I can never marry you, I must marry the sun. Leave this place. If he sees you, he will kill you.'

'Marry me, just for one night!'

She looked at him then, looked at him all over. In those days when we were naked, it was very clear what men were thinking. Her eyes ran over his body, a taut mass of lean muscle (if you like that sort of thing in a man, which most people don't – but she was a spirit and there's no accounting for taste. Besides, he was the only naked man she'd ever seen. Had she had the choice, had there been a naked man in the prime of his life standing next to Arowaku – that is to say, in his early sixties, with a real man's body, not a working man's; that is to say, the sort of body you can get hold of, squeeze, with bits sticking out, an adorable pillow of a man – well, I think we all know which one she would have chosen). As her eyes caressed his naked body, she could see he was ready for her. Her flesh began to tingle, to call out. She smiled. 'Come, come to me,' she called, and lay spread-eagle on a great boulder beneath the falling water. He went to her.

He was her everything, she was his all. They were not two, they were one, their bodies melding, their limbs entangling. Ecstasies building

on ecstasies, flesh against flesh, skin against skin, mortal against immortal, man inside spirit, tongue to tongue, black on silver, one writhing beast, two backs, cries drowned out by the crashing of the waterfall, washing their love juices away.

But dear, gentle reader, the sweeter the fruit, the sooner it rots. The greater the prize, the less the liquorice. As the night began to die, she pushed him away, shouting at him to run, run for his life! The sun was coming. The sun would burn him, would burn everything in his path. She, she was a spirit, she would live, but he, *he* must fly! He ran like he'd never run before, but the sun came after him in a fury, all burnt, and he, Arowaku, the greatest hunter, burnt too.

The moon did marry the sun, but the sun was hot-headed, jealous, furious and cruel. The moon soon ran and hid from him. Even now, from time to time, she sneaks out into the night and looks for her one true love, the mortal man who gave her everything for love. When she doesn't locate him, her tears fall down on the earth, which we find as dew, and the sun then comes and burns them off in his fury.

I normally like pigs. I do not like this *pig. This pig eats babies. Will a baby eat the pig? And how to best insult an octopus, a sea eagle and a very hungry pig?*

The Killer Pig

ong, long ago, all was good and all were happy on the Trobriand Islands. Yams were plentiful, sharks came to be eaten when they were called, coconuts fell from the trees...but into every paradise a snake, or indeed a pig, must crawl. Pigs were (and still are) not normal there. It is a big island and there's lots on it for a pig to eat without disturbing anyone. When gardens were raided and yams dug up, the villagers assumed it was fairies, the Little People – but it wasn't, it was the pig.

As the pig ate, the pig grew. One day as he was snuffling around in a garden he came across a baby in a bag – everything goes in the bag, and normally the baby goes on top of everything, and where else to leave a baby asleep when weeding than gently rocking in a bag? The pig sniffed. The baby smelt good, so the pig grabbed the baby in the bag. The baby cried out and her mother came running, grasping a stick and shouting, so the pig ran off. As this pig could run faster than the mother, he soon disappeared.

I don't know if the pig had originally meant to eat the baby or was only taking it out of curiosity. (I am inordinately fond of pigs and don't want to believe anything bad of them.) I like to think that the pig first fell in love with the baby and wanted to keep it as a pet, but when the baby wouldn't stop crying, he lost his temper and killed it. Then, using his mouth to bash the brains out on a rock, he accidentally tasted blood and found the baby to be absolutely delicious, so gobbled it up. However, as you will see, I suspect this pig

was bad from the word go and the only thing that had stopped him eating babies before was ignorance as to their taste. (But please don't imagine I'm pig-ist or think all pigs are bad and go around killing pigs and eating them simply because of the pig in this story.)

I am sure it is with pigs just as it is with people: some pigs are good and some are bad. But I personally lean more towards pigs and feel most are good; people, I'm not so sure about. Ask yourself this: who would you be most likely to leave a baby with, a stranger or a pig? My uncle Herbert does not like babies at all and he would leave any baby he was given instantly with anyone, anything or anywhere. But most people, I dare say, would be no more likely to leave their baby with a pig as with a stranger. And if they knew the pig but not the person, would probably leave it with the pig (assuming him to be a nice pig, of course. If they knew he was a nasty pig, like the one in this story, they wouldn't...well, not unless they were my uncle Herbert, that is. But I digress.)

I wish this pig had a name, but he didn't, so I'm just going to carry on calling him 'the pig.' Once the pig had eaten the baby and found that it was the tastiest morsel he had ever eaten, quite naturally he munched up as many as he could find. He did manage to find I don't know how many, but soon the word got out and mothers took much more care of their babies, so they got harder to find. The pig, meantime, grew. Being a pig, and therefore smart, he worked out that babies turned into children, and suspected that children were just as tasty as babies. (Here, I think the pig was probably wrong. In far-off days when I ate meat, I once ate a suckling pig at the restaurant St John in London, and it was absolutely delicious. So I suspect if a baby pig is tastier than a young pig, then a human baby is probably tastier than a child. The bones are probably softer and easier to crunch too.)

Children are less easy to control than babies, and as the Trobriands have no predatory mammals and are far from anywhere, children roamed where they liked. The pig tried a child, and finding it to his liking, proceeded to eat many, many more. Children are famously unbiddable and whilst some, probably the girls, might have stayed with their mothers, the boys were not so easily scared. Now, girls do taste much better than boys, or so I've been told. The pig certainly thought so, and thus it was when he was hunting for a young girl that he was first seen. As with every child he ate, he had grown so he was now ginormous.

Warriors pursued the pig deep into the bush. The pig got away, but no one was happy living on an island with a giant pig that ate their babies, so again they set out to hunt the pig. They found him, cornered him, threw spears at him. The spears bounced off his flesh and the pig charged, grabbed one of the warriors by the leg and disappeared. Now, I have every reason to think this was not a civilised pig, not a discerning pig, for he cared not for the quality of the meat, just for the quantity. Once he had eaten this man, he lost his taste for children. I'm not saying he wouldn't still eat a child if he found one, but now he wanted grownups. The more he ate, the bigger he got.

Just when everyone thought it couldn't get any worse, it did. The pig invited his friends, a giant octopus and a giant sea eagle, to join him. Now the villagers were afraid to go to their gardens, because the pig might eat them. They couldn't fish from their boats, because the octopus might eat them. They couldn't go out on the reef at low tide and gather shellfish, because the sea eagle might eat them (not that the pig had left very many people to eat).

The survivors gathered in the sandiest village by the sea (the pig was so big he was scared of sinking in the sand and scared of the fires the villagers kept burning). Knowing that, once their yams ran out, they would starve or be eaten, they prepared their boats to sail away when the winds came again. The pig taunted them: 'You'll never get away,' he yelled. 'You'll never escape! I'll eat you on land and the octopus and sea eagle will eat you by sea!' The octopus lashed the water with his enormous tentacles the size of palm trunks. The sea eagle circled overhead, waiting for someone, anyone, to break the cover of the palm trees.

They decided to leave at night so the sea eagle couldn't kill them. The village magician prepared a powerful spell to disable the octopus – a spell that may or may not have involved a poisoned pig being given to the octopus (which is to say that he told everyone it involved a poisoned pig, but given that there was only one pig on the island, and an eight-year-old boy had just disappeared, I think everyone knew what it was, and thought that it was worth it). Night came; they loaded up their boats. The pig arrived and the pig roared.

He shouted to the octopus to come and get his supper, but the octopus did not answer. He was deep underwater nursing a sore tummy and feeling very sorry for himself. Even if he had heard his friend the pig, which I doubt, he wasn't hungry.

Everyone got into the boats and sailed away. Well, almost everyone, for there was one lady, big with child. Her husband had been eaten, her brother had been eaten, her mother had been eaten. No one seemed to have space for her on their boat, and to be fair, the boats were small and she was large (not that there is anything fair about leaving a pregnant lady to be eaten by a pig, or an octopus, or a sea eagle). Let us hope that everyone assumed there'd be room on the next boat, and for pity's sake, assume that there really *was* no room on the last boat. But she was left alone on the island. Fortunately, the pig didn't see her, and she hid beneath a giant clam shell with her bag of yams.

The next morning she gave birth all alone. She could hear the pig snuffling his way through the abandoned village, knocking over houses looking for food, and she was terrified. She stayed under her shell and nursed her baby. After a few days the pig stopped coming, but still she hid. Then, a cockerel turned up. She said hello, and the cockerel said hello back. The cockerel complained that the villagers had taken all the hens, and he was the only chicken on the island. The woman complained that she was the only person left, and with that, they became best friends. The cockerel would check that the pig wasn't around and keep watch so they both thrived.

When the boy had grown a little and learnt about the pig that had eaten his father and chased everyone away, he said he would go and kill him there and then, he didn't care how big he was. Fortunately, his mother did care and managed to stop him – but she gave him the name of Fearless. Fearless grew and grew, and as he grew, he demanded to be allowed to go and fight the killer pig. However, his mother wouldn't let him and like a good boy, he did what his mother told him to. Then, with one throw of a spear, he split a rock in two. His mother, realising she could control him no longer, said that it was time.

However strong Fearless was, he was not particularly bright. In a straight battle between brawn and brain, brawn will always win, but when you put brawn and brain together, they multiply each other.

So even though the pig was bigger and stronger than the boy, his mother was cleverer than the pig, so she thought they had a chance and devised a cunning plan. She got Fearless to make hundreds of spears. They cleared a spot at the top of a cliff, prepared a fire and left a pile of spears. Climbing down the cliff, they put more stashes of spears up easily-climbable trees. The next day, the boy went alone and lit the fire. The pig smelt the fire and, knowing that food must be on the island, came along trotting happily. He saw Fearless and Fearless saw him. Fearless slapped his buttocks and jeered at the pig. It's hard to insult a pig, but he tried:

'Oy, pig, you're a pig!' (As I've said, he was not the brightest of boys.) 'Your mother was a pig. And your father was a pig.'

The pig himself was not that interested in conversation. He was licking his lips, thinking of his tummy. He muttered back:

'I ate your father and I ate your mother.'

'Not my mother, you didn't!'

'Hmm, she can be next.'

'Come and fight me, *pig*.'

'I'm not going to fight you; I'm just going to eat you.'

The pig advanced. Fearless threw spear after spear. Most bounced off the pig, but some stuck. Just as the pig opened his mouth to grab his breakfast, Fearless leapt down the side of the cliff. Being smaller, he went faster and just managed to climb the first tree ahead of the pig. He rained spears down from his stash. More stuck to the pig, who was furious and smashed himself against the tree, finally knocking him down – but he took Fearless down the cliff with him, giving him a head start as he scrambled up the next tree.

By the time they'd gone through six trees, the pig was looking very much like a hedgehog. Fearless had got some rest in the trees. The pig, however, had exhausted himself knocking them down. Fearless picked up a great spear and drove it in the pig's eye. The pig stumbled and the next spear went into his heart. The pig died.

Fearless had fought like no man had ever fought before and collapsed, unconscious. When he did not come home, his mother knew that he was dead and collapsed in a giant puddle of tears. Her friend, the cockerel, went to check and reported that Fearless and the pig were both dead. She tearfully rushed to bury her son, but finding him still breathing, nursed him back to health, feeding him with huge chunks of delicious pig. With every piece of pig, Fearless seemed to grow bigger and stronger. When he was quite better, he said he'd go into the sea and kill the octopus.

His mother came up with another cunning plan. In open water the octopus was invincible, but in the shallows, Fearless stood a chance. If they could get the octopus's head out of water, he could blind and then kill it. They prepared axes, two canoes and a long bit of rope. In the first canoe they built a couple of stick men. They weren't very realistic, to be honest, but they didn't think the octopus would notice. They attached the canoe to the rope, and at high tide, floated it out in shallow water. In the other canoe were axes and many mighty spears. It didn't take long for a curious tentacle to shoot out of the water. Fearless pulled the boat back into still shallower waters, and so began a long game of 'tease the octopus': whenever the octopus thought he had the boat, the boat would rapidly escape into the shallows. As the game went on, the tide went down. Now, Fearless's mother took the rope and he got into the other canoe.

'Oy octopus, come and fight!' he called out, slapping his arse. 'Your father was a sea snake and your mother was a crab!'

As you can imagine, no self-respecting octopus was going to stand for that sort of abuse. He came into still shallower water to attack the decoy boat. One of the eight tentacles went for Fearless's boat; he chopped it off. An octopus has eight legs and may well be able to regrow them, so the octopus was not worried. Another tentacle came aboard, which was chopped off as well. All the time, the tide was going down and the boats were moving into shallower and shallower water. The octopus's head was now well out of the water.

'You're not an octopus, you're a sea slug! Your mother was a sea urchin and your father was a jellyfish. Come and get me, you great big slug!'

Goaded into a fury, the octopus got closer. Quick as a flash, Fearless sent a spear into each of his eyes. Blinded, the octopus floundered about. Now, Fearless could approach and get a spear into each of the octopus's four hearts. Fearless and his mother then feasted on grilled octopus, stewed octopus, roast octopus, baked octopus and dried octopus.

Fearless's mother had a cunning plan for the sea eagle too. She got her son to make a hole in the bottom of their biggest canoe. They patched it with leaves and mud, then took the longest, strongest dried octopus tentacles – for nothing is stronger than an octopus tentacle when dried – lit a fire and waited for the eagle to notice. Soon enough, they could see him soaring high overhead. Fearless paddled out into the lagoon and yelled, 'Oy, eagle, come and fight me!' He waggled and slapped his buttocks.

The eagle circled and swooped. Fearless capsized the canoe, then broke through the hole they'd patched and called out, 'Your mother was a tree snake and your father was a bat!'

As you can imagine, no self-respecting sea eagle is going to stand for that sort of language. Down he swooped. Fearless retreated into his hole and the talons came in after him. Quick as a flash, Fearless tied them up in octopus tentacles and the eagle was stuck, hobbled, captured. I'd like to be able to say that Fearless swiftly despatched him, but he didn't. Times were different and this eagle had eaten many of Fearless's mother's friends and relations. So he teased him, baited him and insulted him. I could tell you the details, but I won't. Somehow, I feel you can stomach babies being eaten by a pig, but not a man-eating bird being tortured to death, so let's just say the bird died.

When the winds came again, Fearless and his mother sailed off to find the others and tell them it was safe to go home. Then they all lived happily ever after in the Trobriand Islands, Malinowski's fabled Islands of Love.

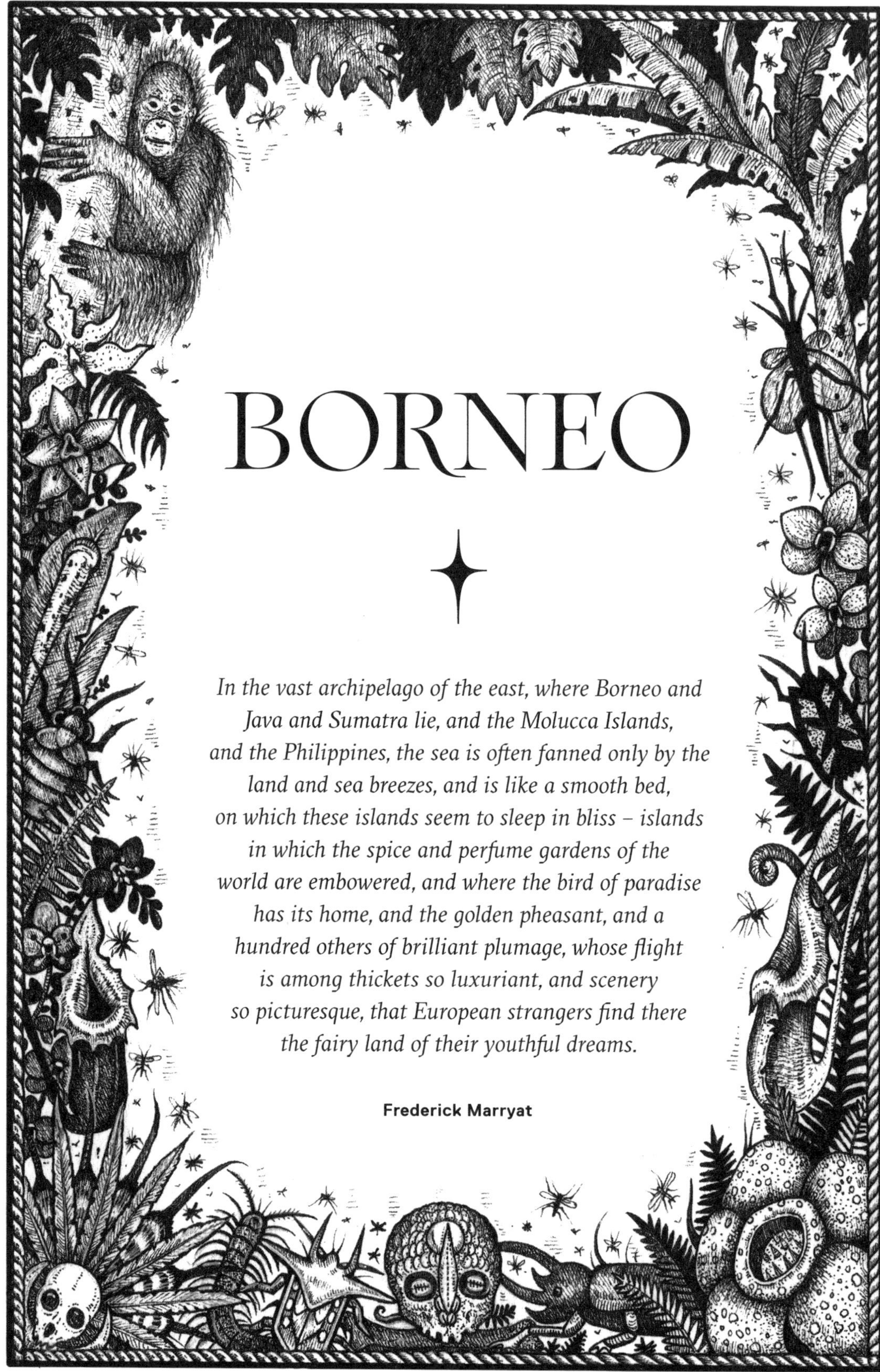

BORNEO

In the vast archipelago of the east, where Borneo and Java and Sumatra lie, and the Molucca Islands, and the Philippines, the sea is often fanned only by the land and sea breezes, and is like a smooth bed, on which these islands seem to sleep in bliss – islands in which the spice and perfume gardens of the world are embowered, and where the bird of paradise has its home, and the golden pheasant, and a hundred others of brilliant plumage, whose flight is among thickets so luxuriant, and scenery so picturesque, that European strangers find there the fairy land of their youthful dreams.

Frederick Marryat

Gentle reader, I want to lie to you; indeed I have *lied* to you. I wrote a beautiful story just for you about a trip to Borneo I took when a student, a long trek and a canoe ride deep into the rainforest, where I stayed in a longhouse, sat at the feet of a wizened chief and learnt his stories. Alas it was all a lie; well almost all a lie. Bits were lifted straight from Redmond O'Hanlon's *Into the Heart of Borneo* and Carl Hoffman's *The Last Wild Men of Borneo* – so there were true stories there, and the only mistruth would be me saying it was *me* and not them. But I read it and I reread it and there was something that didn't ring true, and why lie anyway?

The truth can sometimes be dull, so I'll keep it short. I spend at least a month in New Guinea every year, and my daughters had long been begging me to take them with me, explaining that their greatest desire was to go to a rainforest. New Guinea, however, is a very long way away, it is expensive, it is not particularly safe and lacks infrastructure. Plus, whilst it does have the world's third-largest rainforest, the only mammals it has are very shy nocturnal marsupials. Instead, I thought I'd take them to Sabah in Malaysian Borneo, just two flights away. It's a country with excellent infrastructure and medical care (which came in handy when one daughter broke a tooth and another got a horrible allergic reaction to something in the sea), blessed with incredible and accessible rainforest. We saw orangutans, proboscis monkeys, gibbons, macaques, a pangolin, crocodiles, snakes, green turtles laying eggs and hatching, mangroves, giant flying squirrels, slow loris, Raja Brooke's birdwing butterfly, carnivorous pitcher plants, orchids, tree ferns, scorpions, giant millipedes, spectacular jungle, fireflies and much more.

However, it was the leeches that they saw wriggling and waving at them that the children seem to remember the most, dropping, fat and sated with blood, from my bleeding legs. They *hated* them. Two refused to go into another rainforest, and none now seem that eager to go to the tropics again. We ended the trip with a few days at a very comfortable resort on an island off Kota Kinabalu, where a giant monitor lizard called Gerald sunbathed on our porch, and sharks, barracudas and stingrays could be seen beneath the jetty at sunset.

However, we had been unable to experience any traditional culture. So I thought I'd take everyone to Mari Mari Cultural Village, where various tribes have recreated the longhouses they used to live in (where whole villages or clans resided together in one long building) and demonstrate blow piping, rice wine, textiles and other long-established activities. It was crawling with people and a depressing demonstration of all that had been lost – but sitting cross-legged on the floor in one of the long houses was a traditional storyteller who saved the day. (Not every turd has a pearl, but when it does, it glows brighter for having been born in a turd.) It was from him that I heard the following.

Viktor Wynd
and family
in Borneo,
March 2023

In which a brave hunter wishes he had not married for beauty, a beauty wishes she had spent less time on her back and the whole world becomes a less pleasant place.

The Lazy Housewife's Comeuppance

his tale takes place a long time ago, in the land before time, where life was as never changing as the moon; it came and it went. Long before metal axes, guns and diseases, perhaps just after the clouds had first learnt to cry, it was a time when the veil between the worlds was thinner, and spirits walked amongst mankind. Some will tell you that the spirits regulated the living, rewarding the good and punishing the bad, but I do not know that the good flourished and the bad suffered any more than they do today – that bit may be a moralising fairy tale – however, in those days, the spirits walked boldly amongst the living. Those they did not like, they punished. Those they loved, they rewarded. As it is now, so it was then; looking for a reason for misery or happiness is like looking for patterns in clouds.

One night in a little village far, far away, deep in the rainforest, in the shadow of Mount Kinabalu, a girl was born like no other. Many parents, despite the evidence before their eyes, believe their baby to be the most beautiful thing in the world, but in the case of Loimis, all the villagers were in agreement, all awed and amazed. And as she grew, her beauty only increased – a beauty matched by her intelligence but not, alas, by her diligence. She was never one to help without being asked, to finish a set task or do anything she didn't want to if she could possibly help it.

As she approached puberty and marriageable age, Loimis looked around her and did not like what she saw. Her mother, her aunties and the other village women spent all day working in their gardens, looking after endless babies and children, cooking and sweeping. None of this appealed to Loimis, nor could she see a way out of it. A husband was becoming increasingly needed. She did not want to be dragged into a bush by a man she didn't like and made to do something disgusting with him (something that she thought might be utterly delightful with the right man at a time and place of her own choosing), and then made to marry the rapist and carry on doing it whilst growing food and looking after endless children.

She had one asset, her beauty, and she was determined to use it to buy a different type of life. She resolved to choose the best man for the life she wanted. That man would have to be strong to protect her, an excellent hunter to feed her, hardworking to help in the garden, stupid, so that she could do what she liked and biddable, so that he wouldn't beat her. There was only one obvious candidate for the role: Rutuk. He was totally under the control of his mother, Puntomou, but big, strong and one of the best hunters in the village. He had become a good hunter as an excuse to get away from his mother for days at a time, so that she didn't force him to demean himself by helping in the garden or looking after babies. There were two problems, however. First, Loimis had never looked at him, let alone played with him or associated herself with such an obvious loser in all her life (though, now she came to look at him, she could see that he had the sort of taut, muscular body that she mistakenly associated with pleasure and virility and longed to play with). And second, Rutuk's mother.

People will tell you that, in olden days, what men looked for in a woman was a good wife, broad childbearing hips, strong gardening muscles and an obedient nature. For all I know that may well be true, but men were always, I believe, men, and there is something about beautiful curves, perfect teeth, a smile of joy, deep clear eyes, fine cheekbones, glossy hair and a pair of perfect ski-jump breasts that will always make them stand to attention. So Loimis began to show her charms to young Rutuk, to walk past him, wiggle her hips and smile at him. He was easy. No woman had ever smiled at him like that before, with all her feminine charms, in the days long before the missionaries had told people to cover up, very much on display.

With Puntomou, Loimis was less successful. She pretended an interest in the latest baby and offered to help in the garden, but her help wasn't much good and Puntomou saw through her in a flash. She saw that, like all young women, Loimis wanted her son and chased her away. But Loimis found ways to talk to Rutuk and tell him he shouldn't be living at home anymore; it was time he had a wife. Rutuk was easy to persuade. For the first time in his life he stood up to his mother, who yelled at him, told him he was a fool, that Loimis was a no-good hussy, would be an awful mother and a terrible gardener. But Rutuk was stubborn. As was the way in those days, he built a little house. When it was ready, he carried a very willing Loimis into it, took her maidenhead and initiated her into the joys of love. Meanwhile, the old wise woman in the village taught her ways to mitigate the often unpleasant, not to say terribly fattening, consequences.

As Puntomou had foretold, Loimis was an awful wife, by far the worst wife in the village. However, she was an awful wife in ways Puntomou had *not* foretold. True, she neglected her garden, neglected the house. When the inevitable babies came – for the wise woman could not entirely prevent this calamity, just make it much less common – she neglected them, getting her mother and her mother-in-law, her sisters, her aunties, her sisters-in-law and anyone else to help, whilst Rutuk hunted and did almost all the gardening. But she knew one way to make him happy, one way to give him endless pleasure and forgive her her sins (or rather several ways, all involving going down on her knees). She also knew how to flatter him, to admire him, to make him grumble less, and he was far from blind to the admiration the other men had for his wife.

It may well be that, had he known how to please her the way she knew how to please him, at night when they were on their mat – or in the garden when he got cross with her for lying down and watching him doing all her work and she took him behind a bush and he forgot that he was cross and went merrily back to work – that they would have been very happy and lived happily...but not only is that unlikely, it also would end the story. As it was, he did not know how to please her, or did not please her enough. So when he went off on hunting trips, she started to entertain male visitors at night. If one had finished and she was still hungry for more and another man, or two or sometimes three, just happened to be waiting outside, then she was determined to have her pleasure. If Rutuk were home, or it were daylight and people might see, then perhaps she might go to the gardens to work and accidentally meet a man, almost any man would do, on the way, and pop behind a convenient bush.

The spirits that walked amongst the villagers were not happy. It may be that they were displeased with her behaviour. Or it may be that, in the same way that she neglected her garden and neglected her children, she neglected the spirits and did not make the customary offerings. Whatever it was, her life soured. One night when she was on her mat in her hut and the man on top of her was not her husband, she felt her left shoulder blade begin to itch. No matter: the pleasure on top of her, the pleasure inside her, was greater. She could rub her shoulder on a floorboard and enjoy a good scratch at the same time. Few things give as much pleasure as a truly satisfying scratch. But the itch didn't seem to go away; it got worse. If another man was there and she needed to scratch it and scratch it, she would ask him to scratch it too. To begin with they were happy to scratch her back, for in her own way she was scratching *their* backs too. But the itch began to take over. All she wanted them to do was scratch her back, and that was not why they had crept into her hut in the dark of night. Whenever Rutuk was about, all she wanted him to do was scratch her back.

Now Rutuk, we've said, was stupid. Up until now, he did not seem to care that his wife was the worst wife a man had ever had in every department except the bedroom, but Loimis had always made sure to make him happy in other ways. With her itch, she neglected to pleasure him and neglected to please him with extravagant praise and kisses and cuddles, to sit with an enraptured look on her face when he told her at length about his hunting trip or a long story about his mother. When she stopped doing all this, he realised that the other men's wives grew the food, kept the house, looked after the children and did what their husbands told them. He listened to his mother, who told him, not for the first time, that all the other husbands in the village beat their wives until they did what they were told. He tried beating Loimis, but he wasn't very good at it. Perhaps it might have worked at the beginning, or before the itch had set in, but now the itch was all-encompassing, and Loimis could do nothing but scratch it.

Noticing one day that she'd rubbed the bark smooth on the mango tree by the house with her back, he inserted some very sharp bits of bamboo into the bark and waited to see what happened. Loimis soon returned from the stream, where she'd gone to scrub her back. As she passed the tree, she rubbed against it. The bamboo slices gave her a satisfaction nothing else had and she rubbed and rubbed her back against them, lacerating her skin, staining the trunk red with her blood. She worked herself into a frenzy of rubbing. Alarmed, Rutuk dragged her away. Out of all the cuts a swarm of little insects emerged, small dark bugs half the size of a fingernail. I wish that I could say that the itching stopped, Loimis flourished, became a good wife and lived happily ever after with Rutuk, but alas, I cannot. Horrified, he beat her and chased her out of the village. Somehow or other she found a new village, a new man (or men), and the cycle repeated itself until she'd visited every country on earth, leaving behind her a plague of bed bugs that still flourish wherever slovenly housewives (or indeed slovenly house husbands) neglect their duties.

The great hunter enters the secret valley where he is charmed by beautiful naked maidens, who may or may not be what they seem and who may or may not want to suck him dry. He escapes but brings down an everlasting curse upon the world.

The Blowpiper at the Gates of Dawn

here came a time, as time always must come, when things began to change in Borneo. First came the Chinese men, with strange customs and terrifying weapons, raiding and demanding, trading and taking. Then, a long time later, came rumours of odd creatures, more ghosts than men. But these European men, these monsters, had even more incredible and powerful assets. They were clearly deeply stupid, for, in exchange for valueless things, they would give out enormous wealth in metal axes, cloth and shiny things. For some time in the village these creatures were just unpleasant rumours, another type of bogeyman to be afraid of. Then, the Europeans came to *this* stretch of the Kinabatangan River and the rumours were proved true – some more so, some less so. The wealth they brought was greater than any could have imagined or resisted.

Of all the valueless items the foolish visitors would purchase with their treasure, the one thing they cared about most was birds. Not the edible sort or even the edible bits, just their feathers, which their wives used to decorate their hair (and in the process, almost wiped all the birds off the planet). There was one villager, Sopuk, whose skill with the blowpipe was only matched by his greed and quick intelligence. Soon he was the richest man in the village, with four wives – but, wanting more, he travelled far and wide to get the best feathers. No one had ever crossed the mountain that loomed behind their village. He was convinced that, behind it, he would find feathers of greater value. It took him a long time (well, it might have a been a short time, but I think it was a long time, for it was very far away). He had to climb steep, heavy forested slopes, squeeze through crannies, leap over rushing rapids, scale impenetrable cliffs, and finally, enter a deep cave that came out in a valley untouched by man. The birds there were not afraid. He hardly needed to use his blowpipe; many he could just grab with his hands. The feathers were enormous and extraordinary.

But Sopuk was not alone in the valley; others were there. True, they were not human, but they were there. They watched him from afar; they had never seen the like. When he was asleep, they came to examine him. Never had they seen such beauty, such perfection (and it is true that, for those who like that sort of thing, by which I mean an athletic young man's body, a working man's body, with not an ounce of fat and over-developed muscles everywhere, he was as fine as they come. However, he was the only man they'd seen and I feel sure if they'd seen a real man – by which I mean one approaching the prime of his life, his mid-sixties, with the sort of body that a man who works with his brain not his brawn has, that is to say without many of those nasty hard muscles, and a proper soft, cuddly protruding belly – a *real man* with bits to hold onto, why then, they would not have given him a second look. But his was the only naked male human body that they'd ever seen, and can we blame them for loving it?). When they were sure that he was truly asleep, they put their tiny needles into his flesh and drank deep. They found that it was the most delicious blood they'd ever tasted and took a tiny bottle-full back to their queen.

Once Queen Lojimbong had sampled the ambrosial blood and heard their tale, she had to go and look for herself. As soon as she saw Sopuk, she fell in love. Now, Lojimbong had certain powers. There are some that say that magic changes things and others that say that magic merely changes how we *perceive* things, and that they stay the same but just appear to be different. I do not know which it is, but if I cannot tell, I do not know that it matters much? She transformed her minions into female versions of the man and sent them to him with a summons.

Even though he was asleep, as a true hunter who often travelled in head-hunter territory, he woke up when he heard the faint patter of human steps and drew his knife. He was not prepared for a deputation of the most beautiful women who, unlike those in the villages, had not been influenced by the Europeans and left their charms completely uncovered. They smiled sweetly, bringing him gifts of fruit and delicious morsels of the freshly-cooked flesh of deer. They presented the queen's invitation. Warily, he asked about the king. They laughed and said he was the only man in the valley. He relaxed and followed them to an enchanting palace, larger than any building he had ever seen, filled with lanterns that shone on shiny objects made of the soft, useless yellow metal that he knew the Europeans valued above all else. The walls were draped with silk and doves seemed to coo as though just for him. Queen Lojimbong turned out to be the most beautiful and alluring woman he had ever seen, bedecked with shiny chains, with a glittering crystal star dangling from each ear. She welcomed him warmly.

A feast appeared of every possible delicacy: roast birds, fish so fresh it twitched as he ate it, fruits he had never tasted before. The queen saw him casting his eye about and asked what was missing. 'A drink,' he said. 'No, not water and not juice either.' Puzzled, she wondered what else there could be. She was fairly sure it wouldn't be blood; that was the only drink she herself ever knew. 'No no,' he said, 'not juice and not a coconut either: palm wine.' To blank faces, he explained what it was and then it appeared, just like magic (which of course it was). They all drank deep.

You will know – as I know and they didn't – that those who have never tasted alcohol before are soon overcome by its sometimes delightful effects. All around them, the women started to go to sleep. The queen's eyes bulged. She leered at Sopuk, lunged and pinioned him to the floor. To give him his due, he normally would probably have been very happy to be lunged at and have his flagpole mounted by the queen (even in such a lecherous way, without so much as a by-your-leave). But the alcohol had hardly affected him and there was something so unhuman and cold about her drunken

desire, her greed, that unnerved him, so he pushed her off and she promptly passed out.

Finding himself alone in a pile of intoxicated, unconscious naked women, he decided to explore the palace. It was very odd. The rooms seemed to stretch on forever. It didn't matter which direction he set off in, he always seemed to end up back in the central hall with the drunks. Stranger still, if he then left again by the same door it led to different rooms. On one of his perambulations he found a room full of ceramic storage pots which, to his horror, he found were all filled with blood. Then everything fell into place and, realising he was in the abode of blood-drinking supernatural beings, he turned and fled. Passing through the hall, he took one last look at the most beautiful woman he had ever seen and could not resist taking the queen's diamond earring. He tried to turn her over to get the other, for he was sure the Europeans would give him almost anything for one, but she moved and murmured. Not wishing to risk waking her, he grabbed a handful of golden necklaces and fled.

He ran as only he, the greatest hunter, could run. He did not stop at his village. He followed the river to the sea, and with the enormous sum he got for his feathers, took passage in a great ship heading to the Europeans' home in the far frozen north. Once there, he sold the earring and necklaces for such a vast sum that he was able to set up as a prince in the strange land, where he lived happily ever after.

When the queen finally woke up, or came 'round, and found the beautiful man gone, she was distraught. When she found her earring gone, she was *furious*. Nobody but nobody stole from her! After making them assume their natural winged form, she sent out her followers to find him. They were ordered to bring back the earring and every single drop of his delicious blood; if anyone returned without it, she would kill them. She bred thousands upon millions more and sent them out into the world. I suspect that they are still looking, for I often hear something whining about my ear. And that, my dear, is how mosquitos came out of their hidden valley and why they plague the whole world still.

In which an unhappy barren couple is,
with the help of a little magic, finally blessed
with a baby – but is it really a blessing?

Be Careful What You Wish For

ong, long ago, in the land before time, when the world was young and no one knew that there was a world beyond the high mountains, where the sun set, and where there was but a silly rumour of an endless lake beyond the jungle where the sun rose, life went on as it always went on. Everything changed and everything stayed the same. Babies were born and old men died in the same world their ancestors had lived in. Indeed, their ancestors lived on around them. The missionaries hadn't yet come and banished them all to a burning, bottomless pit of heathens and promised us an ancestor-less land of milk and honey in death if only we'd accept misery in life, a misery caused because some funny men had killed a long-haired, devilishly handsome bearded man in an unpleasant way in a land far, far away, long, long ago. ...Except it turned out he wasn't a man at all and therefore not only hadn't died then, but was still around, and would give you all sorts of things if only you would sing to him one day a week. Weird.

But I digress. In this land there was a girl, a ridiculously pretty girl (not that prettiness counted for much in those days), called Indeela, and two boys that courted her: Hazer, steady and hardworking, and Reehab, who made her very nervous but had something, or everything, that Hazer lacked. In those days, there was little ceremony to marriage. Girls and boys more or less chose who they liked – or rather, boys chose, and once they'd chosen, sometimes they tried with charm, and sometimes they just jumped on the girl if she could be found alone somewhere. The deed done willingly or unwillingly, then the marriage and babies could follow. Not to say that there wasn't much courtship, going for walks together, holding hands and suchlike youthful joys, but a girl had to take care, and Indeela could see that she needed to be very careful of Reehab. Besides, no one else liked her and after something almost happened, indeed probably *would* have happened if she hadn't screamed loudly and her father come running, she realised she needed to make a choice and put Hazer's hand in hers. He would look after her, she knew, and he was a good hunter who could bring food home.

Reehab did not give up. He winked when she passed, and perhaps she might have smiled back a few times, involuntarily but not entirely discouragingly, so he lived on in hope. No one had yet decreed then that marriage was forever, so women sometimes got bored and walked away, men went off with someone else, and of course, people died. Reehab got more and more insistent. One day, he came to her when she was working alone in her garden in the forest. We were naked then, or almost. He waved his magnificent manhood, whirring it around like one of those seeds that spin as they fly through the air, crowing about how much finer, more beautiful and bigger it was than Hazer's. He knew what he was talking about, and she was not as shocked as we would be now. He whirled his lovejoy 'round and 'round and as it twirled, it grew. She looked at it, stared at it; she was mesmerised. She knew that he would not take no, and that if she spent any longer admiring his magnificent, ever-growing manhood, she would not be able to say no either. She backed away. He came forward. She pleaded her growing belly and said she couldn't: she was pregnant. In a fury, he kicked her hard and she miscarried.

She didn't tell her husband what had happened because times were hard then. Perhaps she didn't want the two men to fight. If they had fought, Reehab might have won, and then where would she be? She hated him now. And what if Hazer did not die and was just injured and she was stuck looking after an invalid? No, there was nothing she could do. It was better for the village to live in harmony.

Time went on and her belly would not swell again. When time had passed and passed some more, she went to the village lady who worked with the spirit world and knew which plants helped with which problems. Indeela peed in a pot. The witch smelt it, looked in it, looked at her, muttered things, killed a cock, burnt something and then told her she could never have a child – but it was nothing to worry about, she could find someone else's. In those days, there were always babies and children in search of homes. Mothers died, fathers' heads were taken, disease came and went, children were always going spare, and those without their own were never alone for long.

Except that these two *were* alone. They looked and asked, but no spare children could they find. Their relationship, never very happy, got no happier.

Reehab lurked in the shadows. He told Indeela of the old man, Dunsu, who lived in a cave high up the mountain. The villagers said he was evil, a powerful magician with many strong powers, all for the bad. Reehab said that this was nonsense: Dunsu was a good man with strange powers who just liked to be left alone, but he might help her as she was so very pretty. Even if Indeela didn't really believe him, it was her only hope. She did worry that perhaps Reehab was spinning a web, trying to lure her far from the village in order to jump on her. So she waited until she knew Reehab and Hazer had gone hunting and would not be home for a few days. Then, she walked up and up the river, clambering over boulders through the ravine and up the mountain to the old man's cave.

The ancient, ancient man, his face a spiderless web of wrinkles, greeted her cross-legged from the floor with howl after howl of high-pitched laughter: 'Oh I know what you want, my pretty one, I know what you want, I know what you want, hehehehehehehehe, but you *don't*, oh no, hehehehe, no you *don't* want that, you don't you don't you don't want that! I know what you want but you don't, oh no you don't, you don't want that, hehehehehehe, you don't, no you don't. Be careful what you wish for my dear. You don't you don't you don't want *that*. I can, you can, but do you really want? Hehehehehehe, do you really really want? Hehehehehe, be careful, be very careful what you wish for, hehehehehe you don't you don't you don't. Oh but you *do*, do you? You do, do, do? Well, bring me three cocks and I'll put something inside you and you will you will you will, but don't blame me, *no* don't blame me – *be careful what you wish for*.'

Indeela didn't know what to make of this, but it was her last and only hope. The next time she knew it was safe to visit, she took Dunsu the three cocks. Again, he roared with laughter, 'Oh no you don't, you don't you *don't*, hehehehehe, you really don't. No, you don't want that. But you do, you do you do hehehehehe. If you're *sure* you do, you do, you do but *don't blame me*, hehehehehe! Be careful what you wish for, hehehehehe. Well you've got the three cocks and now I'll put this inside you, hehehehehehehehehe.'

It was when he'd taken the cocks and said, 'I'll put this inside you, get down on all fours like a pig,' that she started to wonder if she'd been had. She was not quite sure what she thought he'd meant when he said he'd put something inside her, but it wasn't this whirling, enormous love sausage growing larger and harder as he twirled it 'round and 'round. Still, it would only last a minute. It never lasted longer, and she wanted a baby. Maybe this would work? So she did as she was told and got on all fours like a pig, but was that really the right hole? Still, Hazer said you had to try every hole, and what did she know? When it did indeed last longer than a minute, she turned to look at the old man. Out of the corner of her eye, she thought she saw Reehab's youthful features in his ancient face, but when she looked properly, it was only the old man's wrinkly, laughing, joyful face. She turned away in disgust, gritted and bore it longer than she thought was possible, until he was done and she could go home, full of hope.

When her belly did not grow and a year and another year passed, she knew she'd been had. Miserable day followed upon miserable day until, one day, an odd thing happened. She'd gone deep into the forest with her husband in search of fruits. The day had already started to die when they heard a crying from the jungle floor and saw a baby where no baby ought to be. They looked around and called, but no one came and there was no sign of a soul. Slowly, hope, and with it joy, blossomed inside her. Perhaps after all she had not been had? They were suspicious at first, but the baby boy was so adorable, so very beautiful. Well alright, they would take it back to the village and see if it belonged to anyone, and if not, and if their wise woman said it was not a spirit child, why then they would keep it – him.

Joy, happiness and love began to flow through their veins. She picked the boy baby up and tried to cuddle it, but the day was dying, and Hazer wanted them to get back before dark. The baby struggled and wouldn't be comforted. It cried and pawed at her breast, but Hazer didn't want to let her suckle it until they got back. But if it was a magic baby, Indeela thought, maybe she would make magic milk. Besides, a breast would calm the baby if nothing else, so she gave it her booby. Never in her life had she felt such an agonisingly sharp, exquisite pain, but she didn't want to cry out. She was sure it was the milk coming; she'd never breast fed before. The pain quickly went and, miraculously, the baby was suckling with a look of such beautiful happiness on its adorable little face that they both fell in love once more and started for home.

Indeela had always struggled to keep up, even when she wasn't carrying a baby. She didn't like to complain at the best of times, so it wasn't until she stumbled and fell that Hazer noticed something was wrong with his wife, was horribly, horribly wrong. There was almost nothing left of her. Her skin was stretched tight over her bones and the baby...well, the baby was enormous. Hazer tried to get it off her breast, forcing open its mouth. Nothing worked, so in a fury he yanked it off, pulling Indeela's breast off with it. The breast hung limp and wilted in the baby's grinning, blood-filled mouth. Furious, he chopped the baby in half with his machete, but it didn't bleed. Instead, out came a mass of strange, dark, slimy, blind, wormlike creatures. He stamped on one and it exploded with Indeela's blood. He squashed more and more, trying to get them all, but some escaped to the river, some to the bushes, some under fallen leaves. All the leeches all over the world descend from that spirit baby. As the old man said, be careful, *be very careful what you wish for*.

HOW TO TELL A STORY

Or: the curse of consumerist society and why you should throw away your television, your Internet, smash your smartphone and make your own entertainment.

We are not machines; we are all storytellers. We tell stories every day. Sometimes, we're just telling people what we did. Other times, we are telling people what we didn't do, but *say* we did. As children, we are all creative. We draw and paint, write stories and poems, sing and dance. Many of us perform in plays, take part in sporting activities. Then, something happens: we (well, I mean *you*, but I don't want to be rude, so I'm including myself here) become boring. We move into a consumer culture where we sit on our arses and watch other people playing football, other people performing on stages, look at other people's pictures, listen to other people's songs, read other people's books. We become slugs. Big, ugly, boring slugs.

It was not always so. The age of mass media, television, smartphones and similar curses has robbed society of much of its innate creativity. They steal our time, they zombify us, they petrify our brains. We become stupider and stupider, content to collapse gormlessly and watch other people do what we could do ourselves. Maybe we can't all play football professionally or paint like Michelangelo, but it is more fun and more rewarding to do it ourselves than to watch others. Doing something professionally doesn't mean you are better at it. At the end of the day, the person who wins the race is just the person who ran the fastest. They've just run as fast as they can. You too can run as fast as *you* can, paint as well as *you* can, perform as well as *you* can.

Just because someone else can do something better is no excuse to do nothing at all, to lounge on your couch watching other people do things. To rest my case: even though you can't fuck like a porn star, that doesn't mean your sex life should consist of watching porn on your phone. You will get more pleasure, have a more meaningful experience having one orgasm with someone else, than you will watching someone on your phone have multiple orgasms with other people. I am not saying STOP WATCHING STOP READING STOP LOOKING. What I am saying is stand up and do it yourself as well. The world does not belong to us, but it is our world, not their world. We shouldn't be mere spectators. PARTICIPATE.

Many of the stories in this book are likely to be as old as humanity. They have been passed down, changed, mutated, abused, improved and performed since Eve first met the serpent. These stories are alive. They shouldn't live in books; books are their tombstones. Liberate the stories and tell them aloud. Learn them, change them, perform them!

There are as many ways of learning and telling stories as there are storytellers. None are right and none are wrong. Here, I am going to tell you how *I* do it:

1 *Find a story you like.*
2 *Think of the story as a map.*
3 *Write down the points in the story where the direction changes.*
4 *Tell the story aloud from your notes.*
5 *Go for a walk with the notes and tell the story to the hedgerows and trees as you pass.*
6 *Go back to your notes and reduce the story to between five and ten points.*
7 *Go for a walk with your reduced notes and tell the story again.*
8 *Go for a walk without the notes and tell the story.*
9 *Keep a notebook with the stories inside. You'll just need to glance at those five or ten points before you tell the story and you'll be off. Names can be difficult to remember, so note them all down at the top, make them up, or don't give them names at all: 'the princess' is just as good as 'Princess Alice' (or name them from your audience).*
10 *And this may be the trickiest bit of all – find an audience. It shouldn't be too hard. Tell your friends, your parents, your cat and your dog. Go to storytelling circles, get grandchildren, find a fire, tell a story.*
11 *Throw away your phone, cancel your broadband, become a part of life. Don't be a couch potato consumerati! Wake up! Become a Real Person.*

The key thing is to think of those five to ten points as places on a map. The storytelling is the walk between each point.

Now you have the story, you can start telling it. You want the story to properly get inside your head so it lives there. The more you tell it, the more the story becomes alive, the more the creatures in it live and breathe. Personally, I plant them on my body as trains. *The Arabian Nights* start on my left foot's little toe with the donkey and the ox and go up my leg to the Brothers Grimm, who start in my testicles with 'The Princess and the Frog' and reach all the way down my left arm and end at my thumb – Tom. My head is filled with

Vikter Wynd's Fairy
Tale Body Map

Irish fairy tales; my tongue is a merrow and my right ear is a corpse. My right arm is Wales, my nipples are Norway, my belly button the one-eyed troll (and the cyclops from Homer). My right leg is Borneo, my big toe a leech, my back is New Guinea. Then, I just start again and have the Mabinogi crawl up one leg, Loki and the Norse gods on an arm, and so on ad infinitum. I have also layered stories on the bodies of past and present lovers, but that's for another day.

The important thing is to place your stories in a landscape you know well. I have put them on the London tube map and given each line a collection. The Northern Line becomes Greenland, the Bakerloo New Guinea, and so on. I have put them in the rooms of houses and buildings I know well, from my prep school to the National Gallery, and now of course I'm putting them in a book. The important thing is to remember them somehow. Don't tell me you have a bad memory. You can always remember whatever it is that is important to you. Yes, it needs a little work, but soon you'll get the hang of it. Nowadays, I can hear a story once and tell it straight away. I can't remember it next week, let alone next year unless I've written it down, on my body, on your body, in my notebook and told it a few times. Give it a try. Please, please, please, I am begging you on bended knees, liberate these stories from the prison of my book! Tell them, let them live.

Example

Now go and read the story. Then, using these notes (that may not always match with the stories as I've written them down in this book), retell the story. Set it free, let it live. Don't worry if it turns into a totally different story. That, my friends, is storytelling.

WALES

Gwen, the Pig and the Witch

1 *Gwendolyn, unwanted love child of farmer and maid.*

2 *Nasty farmer, nasty farm. Beaten and abused, kept with pigs.*

3 *Poor people are at the bottom. Always have been, always will be.*

4 *The farmer's son, Master Evens, tries to rape Gwen and she runs away.*

5 *She has a lovely summer of freedom. She can sense good and bad. Autumn approaches; she needs a place to stay.*

6 *Finds the most beautiful valley on earth.*

7 *Warned to stay away as nasty English farmer, Mr Peak, has chased off the parents and the boy Llewelyn has disappeared.*

8 *Mr Peak is nasty to Gwen, unless she can get the seven golden leaves. Hahahaha, fuck off!*

9 *She walks up the valley. Tree roots become a lovely fairy. Gwen asks about golden leaves.*

10 *Reluctantly told they are wishing leaves from the beginning of time;*

now belong to a witch. Don't *go up the valley!*

11 *She now has a purpose. The first cottage is absolute heaven; lovely old lady. She stays but has to look after pig. Hates pigs.* Never *go up the valley, for that is where the witch is!*

12 *Best time of her life.*

13 *Speaks to pig; pig tells her the lady is a witch.*

14 *Steals the golden leaves. The door and the broomstick pretend to be her.*

15 *Witch chases her on the broomstick. Gwen wishes herself invisible; wishes witch dead.*

16 *Gets to the farm. Everyone there. Mr Peak pleased. 'I wish you'd tell the truth!'*

17 *Mr Peak tells the truth: he murdered the parents, he'll murder the boy.*

18 *Mr Peak hanged.*

19 *Leaves given to fairy. Everyone lives happily ever after.*

You've now told the story once, well done. Now, tell it again using these notes:

1 *Gwen has horrible childhood; runs away.*

2 *Finds magic valley. Boy is missing. Meets farmer and fairy.*

3 *Adopted by lovely granny.*

4 *Talking pig says granny is a witch.*

5 *Takes golden leaves. Kills witch. Boy's uncle speaks the truth; is hung.*

Once you've learnt a few stories, you should get the hang of it. Then, all you will need to do is make the briefest of notes. I can tell all the stories in this book from my notes below:

WALES

The Pooka and the Old Ways

1 *Pooka guide people to copper.*

2 *Christian convinces girl to steal brother's offering.*

3 *No copper. Sister follows brother; makes peace with pooka.*

4 *Copper returns and missionary fed to pooka in nasty way. Happiness.*

Gwion Bach

1 *Orphan asks questions.*

2 *Orphan meets witch; stirs potion for one year.*

3 *Tastes potion. Knows* everything*. Becomes hare, fish, bird.*

4 *Boy worm eaten by witch mole. Witch gives birth to boy; floats him away = Taliesin.*

IRELAND

Bury Me

1 *Ne'er-do-well son must marry Mary. Goes out drinking.*

2 *The Good People tell him to bury corpse by dawn, or else.*

3 *Five churches: at the first, angry*

corpse says no; at the second, ghosts and ghoulies; at the third, make it up; at the fourth, ring of fire; at the fifth, lovely grave.
4 *Marries Mary. Lives happily ever after.*

Love of a Fish

1 *No wife for Paddy. He steals a merrow's cap.*
2 *Marries merrow, is very happy.*
3 *Merrow finds cap in shed; goes home into the sea. Paddy very sad.*

The Good People and a Changeling

1 *Bored Paddy goes to ruined castle on Halloween.*
2 *Joins virgin hunt.*
3 *Steals virgin; virgin's voice taken.*
4 *Goes back for Fairy Liquid. Virgin can speak!*
5 *Eventually takes her to Dublin. Father says, 'Who?' Mum says, 'YOU!' Happily ever after.*

ARABIA

Merchant's Blood (Gazelle, Dogs, Ass)

1 *Merchant sits on baby genie.*
2 *Three sheikhs come.*
3 *Sheikh one, with gazelle, didn't have small balls.*
4 *Comes home. Wife and child gone; kills cow.*
5 *Son is calf. New witch changes back, old witch gazelle.*
6 *Sheikh two, with two brothers who failed as travelling merchants.*
7 *He goes, marries genie, two brothers turned to dogs.*
8 *Sheikh three, unfaithful wife turns to dog. New witch turns wife to donkey.*

Sinbad's Many Many Adventures

1 *Sinbad finds giant egg; gets flown to valley of snakes and jewels.*
2 *Old man climbs on shoulders 'til drunk.*
3 *Shipwrecked. Companions turned to pigs, eaten by cannibals.*
4 *Escapes.*
5 *New place no saddles.*
6 *Marries princess. Princess's sister dies.*
7 *Husband buried with her, his wife dies.*
8 *Escapes from tomb, kingdom where wood is gold.*
9 *Gets home RICH, starts again.*

GERMANY

The Princess and the Golden Ball

1 *Enchanted kingdom. Princess's golden ball rescued by frog.*
2 *Frog comes to lunch; gets into bed with princess.*
3 *Princess adores frog, kisses frog. Frog is a handsome prince!*

Fitcher's Bird

1 *Well-meaning warlock with bad habits seeks loving, loyal bride.*
2 *Test: look after egg; don't go in door or be chopped up.*
3 *First two sisters fail. Third, Elda, succeeds.*

4 *Elda puts sisters in basket with gold and sends home.*
5 *She jumps in barrel of honey, rolls in feather duvet, runs home.*
6 *Fitcher and evil friends burnt to death. There is no such thing as the perfect bride – be happy with what you can get.*

The Juniper Tree

1 *Stepson's head chopped off and father eats him.*
2 *Beautiful bird gets shoes, necklace and millstone.*
3 *Drops millstone on stepmother.*
4 *Stepson comes back to life.*

NORWAY

The Ice Bear

1 *Good king and queen. Two ugly daughters, one beauty.*
2 *Beauty dreams of a wreath; becomes miserable.*
3 *Meets ice bear with wreath.*
4 *He takes her. Bear is great in bed. Sometimes he goes away.*
5 *He takes her three babies. She is miserable. He takes her home for one week; 'Don't listen to your mother!'*
6 *Examines him naked with candle. He goes to troll hag.*
7 *Follows. Magic scissors, flask and tablecloth.*
8 *Climbs the wall, buys three nights with the bear.*
9 *Kills troll hag. Lives happily ever after.*

Three Trolls, One Eye

1 *Two poor boys dream of gold in the hills.*
2 *No gold. Turn back. Woken at night by three trolls and one eye.*
3 *One boy runs, other chops troll's ankle. Eye dropped.*
4 *Boy swaps eye for gold.*

The Serpent Prince

1 *Queen with no male heir told to peel and eat two onions; only peels one.*
2 *Gives birth to snake and boy. Snake thrown in moat. Boy kept.*
3 *A large snake stops prince marrying.*
4 *Snake must marry first, but kills all brides.*
5 *Clever young woman marries wearing seven dresses. Striptease!*
6 *Snake kills brother, becomes king, goes on pilgrimage.*
7 *Nasty princesses pretend queen gave birth to lion.*
8 *King returns. Hidden queen found. Happiness (and of course death – gruesome, bloody, fun!).*

PAPUA NEW GUINEA

Married to Moon

1 *Talk about PNG.*
2 *Jealous husband furious at moon.*
3 *Goes to fight moon at end of long rope.*
4 *Fails, comes home.*

The Discovery of the Moon

1 *Talk about Sepik.*

2 *Scorned hunter digs up massive kina.*

3 *Kina, spirit of moon, floats away.*

4 *Finds her again. They bonk under waterfall.*

5 *Jealous sun kills him.*

6 *Moon hides, and sometimes looks for him and cries.*

The Killer Pig

1 *Giant pig, octopus, sea eagle.*

2 *Everyone leaves except pregnant woman.*

3 *Child grows up to be Fearless.*

4 *Fearless kills pig.*

5 *Octopus killed in low water.*

6 *Sea eagle killed with hole in canoe.*

BORNEO

The Lazy Housewife

1 *Beautiful lazy housewife chooses stupid, dependable lover over dangerous lover.*

2 *Sleeps around. Fools stupid husband.*

3 *Starts to itch.*

4 *Sharpened bamboo in mango tree – out come bed bugs. Chased from village and spreads them across world.*

The Blowpiper

1 *Blowpiper hunting for feathers in distant valley, woken by naked ladies.*

2 *Palace beautiful: queen, feast, women get drunk.*

3 *Finds jars of blood. Terrified. Steals earring, runs away.*

4 *Queen is a mosquito. Sends mosquitos out into world to get earring.*

Be Careful

1 *Indeela chooses good man Hazer. Bad man Reehab hangs around; kicks = miscarriage.*

2 *No baby. Indeela goes to warlock. 'Be careful what you wish for!'*

3 *Goes back with offerings; gets fucked. Still no baby. Unhappy.*

4 *Indeela and Hazer find baby in forest. Very happy. Baby sucks her dry. Hazer cuts baby open; leeches come into the world.*

NOTES

NOTES

NOTES

NOTES

NOTES

NOTES

NOTES

NOTES

ABOUT THE AUTHOR

Viktor Wynd is a 'pataphysical artist and chancellor of the Last Tuesday Society in London. He has been performing the stories in this book to audiences small and large around the world for the last twenty-five years. He is the author of two books previously published by Prestel, *Viktor Wynd's Cabinet of Wonders* (2014) and *The UnNatural History Museum* (2020).

Born and raised in Muswell Hill, London, he studied French at the Sorbonne in Paris, Islamic history at London's School of Oriental and African Studies, and Fine Art at The John Cass (as it was called then) and the University of South Florida, where he held the James Rosenquist Fellowship while studying for an MFA.

His solo art exhibitions have included *Why I Think I'm So Fucking Special* (OBJEX Artspace, Miami, 2004), *Structures of the Sublime: Towards a Greater Understanding of Chaos* (Ingalls & Associates, Miami, 2005), *The Sorrows of Young Wynd* (Ingalls & Associates, Miami, 2005), and *The Infected Museum* (The National Maritime Museum Cornwall, Falmouth, 2020–2022).

Since 2009, he has been collaboratively creating an immersive world in London's East End: The Viktor Wynd Museum of Curiosities, Fine Art & UnNatural History, a twenty-first-century *wunderkabinett* and *Gesamtkunstwerk* replete with exhibitions, lectures, and an absinthe parlour. In 2018 he founded Gone with the Wynd, a tour agency specialising in biannual trips to New Guinea and West Africa. He lives on a small farm in Suffolk with his wife, four children and an ever-growing menagerie.

ABOUT THE ILLUSTRATOR

Luciana Nedelea is a Romanian archaeologist, historian and artist who received her PhD from Babeș-Bolyai University of Cluj-Napoca. She has published numerous articles on history and archaeology, as well as chapters and collected volumes (including *Tabula Imperii Romani – Forma Orbis Romani: Dacia*, published by The Romanian Academy, for which she served as editor and co-author). She has participated in various national and international conferences, research projects (such as *Dacians in the Roman Empire: Provincial Constructions*), and archaeological campaigns.

As an artist, she has collaborated with researchers, authors, publishing houses, event organizers, musicians/bands and private collectors worldwide. She is known for her work in the heavy metal industry (primarily Black Metal), specializing in traditional, hand-drawn designs for bands including Altar of the Horned God, Dark Funeral, Fuath, Griefspell, Ghost Bath, Grá, Grifteskymfning, Kalmankantaja, Mare Cognitum, Nightbringer, Scáth na Déithe, Walghinge, Witchtower and many others.

She has also designed merchandise for the religious organization The Satanic Temple, based in the US. Some of the original artworks for these designs are permanently exhibited at the TST Salem Art Gallery. In 2018, she had a solo exhibition organized as part of the Transilvania International Film Festival, where she was also selected as a jury member in the Shadows Shorts Competition.

Viktor Wynd: To the storytellers, writers, poets and drunks who recognise their words, their stories in this text: thank you. I'd thank you individually if I could remember all your names or remember where I first heard or read a story. If you recognise your words, it is because they are good words.

I've been telling stories since I was a child. All children tell stories. Some reach puberty and stop. The rest of us carry on and either become criminals or con men and get called liars, or become artists and get called dreamers. Thank you for listening.

Thank you to my first audience, who gathered on the roof of the Benaki Hotel in Athens in 2003. To every audience ever since, to everyone who ever came – and, indeed, left.

Thank you to the Suffolk trees and hedgerows, who have listened to all my stories as I wander. I must thank my daughters Leonora, Phoebe and Daphne, who have been listening to fairy tales since they were born.

I must go down on bended knees and thank Leonora Carrington, who showed me that the world of magic, of fairy tales, is not just a child's world.

Thank you to Andrew Hansen at Prestel, who first encouraged the idea of this book (over rather a good lunch). To the most extraordinary and wonderful editor, Ali Gitlow, who wrote to me long ago (two books ago, to be exact) asking if I'd ever thought of writing a book about myself, who takes ideas and different people and turns them into magnificent books. Nothing would happen without an editor. It is the editor's name that should be on the cover, in neon lights a mile high.

Thanks to Lauren Humphries-Brooks, for copyediting and proofreading, and designer Benjamin Wolbergs. Also, a big thanks to the publicity team at Prestel, who are going to do such an amazing job of telling everyone about this book and are the only reason why you are reading it now.

Thank you to Clare Conville and Elizabeth Milne at C&W Agency for your support.

When it came to illustrating this book, I wanted to do the drawings, I wanted to use old illustrations, I wanted to use old photos, things from my scrapbook. Ali wanted an illustrator. It took us months of back-and-forth and then we asked Luciana. A huge thank you to Ryan Matthew Cohn for introducing me to her work. I'd admired it for years on Instagram and had bought a few drawings that I really love; one hangs next to my bed. There is something magical and dark, but at the same time quite funny, about her work. Her references are my references. We love and are steeped in medieval history, storytelling and the macabre. She knows many of these stories better than I do, and through her pen has brought them to life. I go down on bended knees and thank her here. I hope you like her drawings as much as I do (even if the originals don't hang in your house as they hang in mine. Lucky me).

Luciana Nedelea: I would like to thank my wonderful parents, who always believed in me, allowed me to be true to myself and to pursue my dreams. I owe everything to their caring upbringing, focused on education, culture and individualism, despite living in a post-communist country.

Besides my parents, I am much obliged to the first person who taught me the basic principles of art at age fifteen: Professor Adina Mocanu of the Bistrița-Năsăud Arts High School (also known as "Corneliu Baba").

I would like to thank all individuals who trusted me with creating their designs over the years. Without you, my work would not have seen the world, in the truest sense of the word. For that, I am eternally grateful!

It was always a dream of mine to fully illustrate a book, and when the opportunity to work with Viktor Wynd on such a wonderful project arose, I just knew that it was meant to be. I have always admired Wynd for his eccentricity, sense of adventure and exploration, dark humour and interest in the occult and all things horror. He is truly a man before his time. I thank Wynd immensely for choosing my art to accompany his wonderful adventures, and I look forward to meeting for a glass of absinthe one day!

Last but not least, I would like to thank Prestel Publishing and the amazing Ali Gitlow, without whose impeccable directions, patience and collaboration all this would not have been possible. Thank you, dear Ali, for all your wonderful work!

© Prestel Verlag, Munich · London · New York
A member of Penguin Random House Verlagsgruppe
GmbH, 1st Edition, 2025

produktsicherheit@penguinrandomhouse.de

A Library of Congress Control Number is available.

A CIP catalogue record for this book is available from
the British Library.

Editorial direction: Ali Gitlow
Copyediting and proofreading: Lauren Humphries-Brooks
Design and typesetting: Benjamin Wolbergs
Production: Luisa Klose
Origination: Reproline Mediateam, Munich
Printing and binding: TBB, a.s., Banská Bystrica
Penguin Random House Verlagsgruppe FSC® N001967

Printed in Slovakia

ISBN 978-379-7913-9350-6

www.prestel.com

Viktor Wynd's
Fairy Tale Map
of the
World
Norway
Canada
Wales
Ireland
Germany
Amazonia